No Light at the End of the Jungle

By

Jerry Wood

ISBN: 1-4107-1329-6 (Electronic)
ISBN: 1-4107-1330-X (Softcover)

This book is printed on acid free paper.

1stBooks - rev. 01/15/03

PRELUDE

The mid day sun beat down hard on the human train of a hundred and eighteen of us as we were being pushed and prodded through a trail cut into the dense jungle. Our captors, numbering about a dozen, poked and jabbed at our scrawny and exhausted bodies, forcing us to continue on our trek north. We stumbled along the trail as if we were zombies in a movie, expressing no will or emotion toward our out numbered guards.

As we reached a sharp bend in the trail a shrill voice rang out, "NOW!" and I knew it was time. I and a handful of others had made a vow not to live as we had anymore, and if death was the only alternative, then so be it.

Simultaneously eleven extremely undernourished men, weakened by the savage beatings they had received over the last year and a half, bolted for the jungle. Time seemed to slow to a crawl as if I were suspended in slow motion, and I wondered if I would ever reach the edge of the jungle which was merely steps away.

Only a few feet into the foliage I realized that the vegetation was so dense that it would be impossible to get through it without a machete. Automatic gunfire behind me began to penetrate the solid wall of green with muffled thuds, and I could hear the guards yelling back and forth in their high pitched language. Some were scrambling after the hopeful escapees and the others were trying to regain control of the remaining prisoners.

I fell to my knees and began to scratch my way under and around the foliage as if I were a snake slithering through the grass. I worked feverishly, burrowing my way as deep into the jungle as I could. Feeling the strength draining from my body, I willed my hands and legs to keep moving, digging and clawing my way to freedom. The thought of what would happen if caught made my whole body tremble. There would be no inhumane beatings as before; this time the sentence would be death.

Behind me I could hear a couple of the guards yammering their sing-song gibberish and wielding their machetes, cutting a path into the jungle. Suddenly their voices stopped and a barrage of bullets from their AK-47 rifles echoed through the jungle. I froze, trying not to even breathe. My heart was pounding so hard that I was sure it was as loud as the shots being fired.

A loud moan came from somewhere to my left, and the shots stopped. The guards again began cutting through the dense greenery, directing each other to the sound of their injured prey. One of them stopped about six or seven feet from where I lay and sang out that he had found their quest. My stomach came up into my throat, as I lay there completely motionless. When the other guard reached that spot, I could hear the thuds of their bayonets finding their way deep into the chest of their quarry, and then the whimpers of a dying man. After a brief exchange of snide remarks and a chuckle or two, the two guards turned and retreated back along the path they had cut during their search.

I could hear the frenzy of the guards regaining control of the remaining POWs, as the officer in charge bellowed commands to his troops. One of the returning guards reported to his superior in his native gibberish, most of which was indistinguishable to me except his last two words, "chet het (All dead)". The officer in charge accepted the report then turned and began yelling out more commands to his troops. Soon the gaggle of men embarked once again on their march to Hanoi and their sounds began to grow faint.

"All dead." The guard's words echoed through my head like thunder. I began to sob and my whole body trembled at the thought that everyone had been killed but me. The sorrow of the loss of my companions overwhelmed me and I lost control of my sobbing. In all our planning I hadn't prepared myself for being the only one to survive.

Suddenly the sound of someone scurrying through the jungle toward me broke through the sound of my whimpers. "Oh my God, they came back," I thought. To no avail I tried to silence my weeping and regain control of myself.

"Hey, who's there?" Came a whispering yell.

The voice was American, someone else did make it! The guards were wrong! When I tried to respond, my emotions were a mass of confusion and I could only sob louder. After a few minutes the voice reached where I lay.

"Shush, shush. You alright? You hit?"

As I looked into the face of the man crouched in front of me, my heart filled with joy. Although I had only seen his face for the first time two days ago I knew him well. I had learned all about him and he me, over the last year or so. I had communicated with him daily even though as POWs we were caged in isolation and forbidden to speak. This person was the source of all my strength and gave me the will to go on and live during the time of my incarceration.

This man's name was Alan and he was the toughest person I have ever met.

CHAPTER 1

In the early sixties the U.S. Government was becoming more and more involved in a police action called "Vietnam". For me, however, I don't remember any awareness of Vietnam until the time came for me to go there. I had more important matters to be concerned with, or what I, as a young high school student, thought were more important. During those early years it was impossible for me to know how this "police action" would affect my life, and therefore world events weren't something that concerned me.

I was raised by my grandparents on a small farm in eastern Washington, and up till the age of about twelve or thirteen my main concern was being sure the few cows we had were milked every morning before school. At about age thirteen my granddad had his third heart attack, which forced him into selling the farm and us to move to town. Now having fewer chores at home I became active in sports at school. My granddad was a very big baseball fan and the fact that I excelled in baseball made him proud. It even made him prouder when in my senior year of high school it became evident that I would possibly play professional baseball some day. Before each game my granddad would urge me to give every game my best.

After practice one day, toward the end of the season of my senior year, the coach called me to his office. "John," he began," as you already know, we're going to go to the state championships this year. And these last couple of games are going to be the biggest and most important games of your high school career."

"Haven't you said that every game is important, coach?"

"Yes I have, but these games aren't only important to the team, they're really important to you. You're going to have to make some important decisions after these games."

"What kind of decisions?" I asked.

"Well, I was going to wait a week or so before I told you this, but I think it's important you know now. WSU (Washington State University) and Arizona State are going to offer you a scholarship in baseball."

"All right!" I interrupted.

"Also," he continued, "I have some inside word that at these next couple of games there is going to be a couple of pro scouts there looking at you." I was somewhat stunned by this revelation, as playing pro was my biggest dream. The coach continued, "Both, the scholarship and turning pro have good and bad points. I think you need to talk to your family about what will be best for you and if you like I'll be happy to join your discussion to explain the good and bad points and all your options."

All I could say was, "Wow!"

"You've got a lot to think about here, so go home and talk to your grandparents, then tomorrow let me know if they would like me to come by and talk to all of you."

That day I went home and told my grandparents what my coach had related to me. They both were elated, but for different reasons. My grandma wanted me to go to college and grandpa liked the idea of going pro.

Over the next several weeks my options and decisions were the topic of many discussions. Our team won the state championship and I received the most valuable player award. I had two scholarships and a pro contract offered to me and it was time to make a decision.

Only one time did the word Vietnam ever come up, and that was back when the coach sat down with us to go over my options. One statement was that the scholarship would defer me from the draft and Vietnam. That subject never came up again or was even a consideration in my decision.

After a considerable amount of coaxing from my granddad and myself, grandma finally gave in to the fact that maybe I would become a superstar in the pros. A pro contract was signed and after an early graduation I was on my way to spring training, and on my way to stardom, or so my granddad and I thought.

2

I worked hard during spring training and was on my way to play in the Texas League. However, for the first time I had the experience of not making the starting line up.

Soon after the start of the season I met Linda, a beautiful young girl, with golden blond hair and big blue eyes. It didn't take long before I knew I was falling in love with her. We began to spend every possible moment we could together even though I would be gone for periods of a week to ten days at a time playing road games, or should I say sitting on the bench for road games. It wasn't possible for her to travel with me because back then we traveled as a team on a bus and stayed in second rate hotels, also back then I sure wasn't getting the big bucks that I had envisioned.

A little over half way through the season, Linda told me she was pregnant. This came as a surprise but was not upsetting. I knew that I loved her and wanted to spend my life with her so the solution was easy. We got married and for our honeymoon I went on an eleven game road trip. Despite not having much money and my frequent road trips, we were young, in love and very happy.

Up till the end of the season, Linda and I couldn't have been happier. Soon we would have a baby and I was sure that the next year I would make the starting line up. The latter, however soon would be shattered. At the end of the season, since we hadn't made the playoffs, we were clearing out our lockers for the off season, when the general manager called me to his office.

"Hey Red," I greeted him as I entered his drab little office. "Next year we'll be better, don't you think?"

"Yeah kid, sit down." He started. "Kid this is the toughest part of my job." He paused and with a sad expression continued, "We're going to release you kid."

"What do you mean release me?" I responded with pure shock.

"Well kid, the team has decided to bring in this new kid from the rangers and I just don't have a spot for you on the roster. I'm sorry, but that's the way it is."

"What happens now?"

"Well kid, your contract has a cut clause in it, which means if your released you get, oh, I think it's about eight or nine thousand dollars plus your final pay. You come around to my office tomorrow afternoon and I'll see to it that you have your check. Ok?"

I left his office devastated. All my dreams now were gone. "Now what?" I thought. I've got a family to support and no college education, as I turned down the scholarships, and now no star bound career. How was I going to tell Linda, and what was she going to say?

I received just a little over ten thousand dollars for the cut clause in my contract and my final pay. Even though that amount was a lot of money for back then, especially for an eighteen-year-old kid, I knew it wouldn't last long. Within a short time I would have a large medical bill for the birth of our baby, and living expenses on top of that. Linda wasn't really upset about me being cut from the team, but was concerned about our future.

One afternoon, while I was out trying to find work, I happened to walk by an office building with a big sign in front. The sign was a picture of "Uncle Sam" saying he needs you or something to that effect. The next thing I knew I found myself setting inside talking with a recruiter. After talking for a while he told me that I could get out of the draft one of two ways.

First, I could apply for a deferment because of being married and having a baby on the way. With this deferment, I would probably not have to serve in the military at all. Taking this option, however, seemed to go against everything that my granddad had taught me. The second option, to join the Army before I was drafted, had a lot of benefits, the biggest of which was the medical. Some of the other benefits were a steady income and the choice of what I wanted to do in the military. The recruiter gave me a lot of pamphlets to read over and suggested that I take them home, read them and discuss everything with my wife.

That evening Linda and I discussed all the aspects of joining the Army. She liked the idea of the medical, especially for the baby. "Also they have a program where I could be a pilot." I interjected. "All the other branches of service, you have to have a college degree."

"Yes, but what about having to go to Vietnam?" She asked.

"Oh, I don't know. I guess I might have to go, but that's just part of the price everyone has to pay in the service of their country." I answered.

"I don't know John." She responded. "I'm not sure I believe in Vietnam. All my friends say it's a bad thing and we shouldn't even be there."

"Linda, I have to believe that our government knows what they're doing. We have to fight wars on foreign lands in order to keep it safe and free here at home."

"But I don't know if I would want you to go to war." She added.

"Oh honey. First of all, we don't know if I would even have to go. Second if I did, nothing would happen to me as a pilot. The ones that got it tough in war are the infantry men." I explained to her.

By bedtime we had decided that the next day I would once again talk with the recruiter. If he could assure me of pilot training I would join the U. S. Army.

CHAPTER 2

Linda moved in with her parents while I was in boot camp. Her parents would bring her to see me on the weekends and I would call her on the phone every evening. At the end of boot camp I was given a thirty-day leave before I was to start flight school. During this time little Richard was born.

Flight school was to be nine months long. The first part, four months, was at Fort Walters, Texas, where I again would have to live on post in the barracks. The second phase of five months was at Fort Rucker, Alabama, where I would be allowed to live off post with my wife and new son.

I graduated at the top of my class and at graduation received my wings and the rank of Warrant Officer. Also, at this time we received our orders. The vast majority of my class was headed for Vietnam; however I received orders for AMOC (Aviation Maintenance Officers Course) in Fort Eustis, Virginia. At the end of my training in Virginia, I once again was given a thirty-day leave and orders for Vietnam.

Upon my arrival in Vietnam I was immediately transported to my unit, the First Air Cavalry Division, in Anke. Once there I was given a short indoctrination and sent to the field in Bon Sung. Here, I was given a one-day orientation flight and immediately assigned to fly missions. I soon found myself as just one of the guys and the daily realities of war became routine.

One of the great joys in Vietnam was receiving mail. It was something you looked forward to every day and Linda didn't let me down. I received a letter from her almost every day and on the days I didn't receive a letter, I would receive two the next day. In one of her first letters she informed me that she was once again pregnant and we were now expecting our second child. This news made me happy but also it made me sad that I wasn't there.

Becoming acclimated to Vietnam came quickly. You were forced to become a seasoned veteran with daily doses of the realities of war. At night you were always on alert for a motor attack and during the day you would be in contact with the mangled bodies of young soldiers who really knew the perils of war. After only a month in Vietnam I became an aircraft commander. No longer was I a FNG (fucking new guy) assigned to other seasoned pilots. I now was a seasoned pilot, an old-timer, and had the FNGs assigned to me.

As an aircraft commander you were always on alert to the actions of your young new copilots. You never knew how anyone, including your own self, would react to a combat situation. Many times going into or coming out of a hot LZ (a hot LZ is a landing zone where the enemy is shooting at you) with bullets flying everywhere and slamming into the helicopter, my copilots froze up or began crying and screaming. Everyone reacts differently to fear, and fear is a powerful force that is hard to control. However, sometimes a person will react completely opposite to what you would think. For example, I had a new pilot, we called Grasshopper, assigned to me. He got the nickname of Grasshopper because he was skinny and had the longest legs I think I've ever seen. Anyway, we were inserting troops one day into a hot LZ. Bullets were flying everywhere, with our red tracers clashing with the enemy's green tracers, creating a fourth of July fireworks display. As we were leaving the LZ, Grasshopper was flying, a round came through the windshield and struck him dead center of his chicken plate (we wore armored vests which were called chicken plates). Some of the chicken plate splintered and sent a few pieces into his neck area cutting him about the same as if you cut yourself shaving. I quickly came alert expecting him to come unglued and I would have to grab the controls. He never did however, he just continued to fly calmly as if nothing had happened. After a short time his calmness was driving me crazy. I finally told him I had the aircraft and took control flying us back to base camp. Twenty minutes later we landed and got out of the aircraft. I was about to tell him how tough I thought he was when he took off his chicken plate, then held it up and looking at it he turned ghostly white and fainted.

It's ironic how you always try to make your surroundings more civilized. During my tour in Vietnam we lived in tents surrounded with sandbags, the sandbags gave some safety from motor and rocket attacks, and slept on an air mattress, which was on psp (metal panels used in the construction of runways) placed on a couple sandbags. At any rate, one day we had flown some other pilots down to Quen Yon to pick up some new helicopters. Once there, Bradley, my copilot, said, "Ya know I'm sure tired of living in a tent." I laughed and asked what that was supposed to mean. He pointed to a bunch of plywood stacked up at the end of the runway and said, "With that we could build us a nice little hooch and live somewhat like humans."

Before I knew it he had conned some GIs there into loading the plywood aboard our aircraft. Once we were back at our base camp, with the stolen plywood, we used some ammo crates as studs, and erected a nice four-bunk hooch.

It was great to have real walls around us instead of canvas, even though it only lasted a short time. Soon after moving into the newly erected hooch, we found ourselves headed for the bunkers as we were under a motor attack. In the vast majority of motor attacks the enemy aims for the revetments guarding the helicopters, however on this rare occasion one round found its way away from the flight line and was a direct hit on our castle. This fate ended our attempts to improve our living conditions.

After being in country for about four months the Army had a program where a person could apply for a direct commission. I decided to apply, since it meant more money, and was granted a commission from warrant officer to first lieutenant. This promotion however didn't lighten my mission load. We always had more missions than pilots.

One late afternoon, after flying a hard run of missions, I returned early looking forward to a couple extra hours of rest. However, it was not to be as the operations officer sent for me. "Listen Walker," He began, "We got the general here today and he wants to take his staff up and look at this area over here." He smiled at me as he pointed to a spot on the map.

"Ah, no. Come on." I responded.

"Hey, you're all I have right now." He retorted.

"Ah shit, all right."

I flew the general and his staff to the area he wanted to see and pointed out the aspects I was suppose to. The general informed me he wanted to get a closer look and I told him that the whole area was full of VC and getting any closer wasn't such a good idea.

"Lieutenant, it looks safe enough to me, let's get a little closer look." He ordered.

I was too tired to argue and knew I wouldn't win anyway, so closer we went. Instantly we began taking enemy fire and one round struck the engine. I quickly began my autorotation to a near by rice patty and radioed a "may day" call with our location. The one good thing about having a general on board, was that I knew help would be there in no time. I told the gunners that once we touched down pull the M60 machine-guns off the aircraft and take up a position on the levee of the rice patty which I was trying to get close to. Once on the ground, everyone scurried off the aircraft on the side of the levee. The general, however, got off the helicopter on my side, the opposite side from the levee, and began to walk upright to the front of the aircraft. I grabbed my rifle, which I carried in addition to my 45 pistol, and not knowing the general was by my door, I kicked open the door. As I was scampering from the aircraft for safety, I knocked the general face down into the muddy bog of the rice patty. It was like in a cartoon, he was covered from head to toe with mud. In no time at all there were gunships flying overhead returning fire on the enemy and two slicks landing to pick us up.

Shortly we were landing back at base camp and as I was exiting from the aircraft, which I flew back on, the general, who had been on the other helicopter, was walking toward me. I thought to myself, "Oh man, I've done it now. I'm really in for it big time."

The general, caked with mud, walked up to me and I came to the position of attention as he said, "Lieutenant, I didn't realize the situation out there. I just want to thank you for saving my life."

Stunned by his words, "Why yes sir. Your welcome sir." I answered as I laughed to myself. I wasn't trying to save his life, I couldn't have cared less about him. I was just trying to get to safety myself. I wasn't going to tell him that, however, so I received the Silver Star.

Halfway through my tour, word came that our sister company, a gunship company, was critically short pilots. With the opportunity to

Jerry Wood

fly the new Huey Cobra (AH-1G) helicopter I transferred. Soon I was happy to learn that as a gunship pilot the tragedies of war were less visible. The daily doses of wounded soldiers were no longer part of my daily routine. It would not be long, however, that I would be part of a mission where I would learn first hand the perils of war.

CHAPTER 3

It was toward the end of my tour in Vietnam that I was shot down and captured. My unit, the First Air Cavalry Division was now assigned to Hue - Phu Bai near the demilitarized zone. We were preparing to insert a massive number of troops into the Ashau Valley where a huge assault was to take place. The plan was to disrupt the use of the Ho Chi Mien Trail, used by the Vietcong as a pipeline for all of their supplies and troop replacements. The brass, however, made a large miscalculation of the enemy strength and size and of the ability of the Vietcong to mount a jungle warfare counterattack.

My company's assignment was to escort and provide cover for the main body of troop-carrying helicopters called slicks. Since my company was a gunship company, my job as a gunship pilot was to lay down cover fire allowing the slicks to land in the landing zone, unload troops, and take off again. I had flown missions of this type before and many times had received enemy fire. This mission, however, would prove to be beyond anyone's wildest nightmare.

Twenty minutes prior to the LZ (landing zone) time the artillery base began an onslaught of fire canvassing the entire LZ area, and the rain of shells would last for fifteen minutes. The purpose of this was, like always, to drive the Charlies (Vietnamese Gorillas) out of the area and allow the troops to be inserted without incident. There again, I don't believe the brass realized how well Charlie was dug in and how bad they didn't want us in that area.

Our flight of Huey Cobras rendezvoused with the main body of slicks (UH1H helicopters used as troop carriers) three clicks southeast of the LZ at check point Alpha, and established initial contact. "Raincloud Leader, this is Red Flight Leader. Your escort has arrived. Over." Raincloud responded and gave our flight commander a last minute update saying they would be landing to the north and we were to proceed with cover as per our preflight briefing. "Roger, Raincloud. Red Flight, did you copy Raincloud?" Each pilot in sequence rogered that they had heard and understood Raincloud. "All right, Red Flight, change to tac one and acknowledge." Each aircraft was equipped with two UHF radios. One was set to the frequency that we were on and would be used by the main body to coordinate that part of the mission. We would monitor that frequency but tune the other radio to a different frequency to coordinate our own portion of the mission. I turned my dial and responded, "Red Two's up," and the rest of the flight did the same. "Roger, Red Flight, break off and take positions as instructed in preflight." Each bird rogered and took its position.

The flight was flying in an upside down "V" formation with the point of the formation being Red One. Our preflight briefing called for Red One, Two, and Three to go in ahead of the main body and strafe the LZ and both sides. Red Four and Five would come in on the flanks of the main body, even with the main body lead and do the same. Red Six and Seven would be on the flanks but in trail and just provide fire where needed. After the first five birds made their run we were to break off and provide cover fire wherever directed.

"Red Flight, Red One will begin run in thirty seconds."

"Red Two's with you."

"Red Three's with you."

"Red Flight, arm weapons systems now."

With our weapons systems armed, we began our run on the LZ. I squeezed the trigger on the cyclic and my miniguns immediately responded by laying down a pattern of fire covering the entire left side of the LZ. To my right I could see the spray of bullets from Red One and Three joining with mine to sweep the entire area. As we were completing our run, Raincloud Leader announced that he was on short final. I released my trigger and pulled back on the cyclic beginning a climb as I banked to the left.

Red Three came over the radio first. "Red Three taking heavy fire eleven o'clock!" Then came, "Red One's got heavy fire. Red Two, can you pump rockets to my twelve o'clock at source?"

"Red Two, that's a roger."

I quickly pulled the cyclic back to the right and at the same time armed my rockets. As I banked right I could see green tracers flooding the sky coming from north of the LZ. I began to punch off my sixteen pound warheads, directing them to the source of the tracers and also realized that I was now taking fire from my left. Pressing my radio switch, "Red Two's taking fire from my three o'clock. Four, can you hit them?"

Red Four, who was to my rear, came back, "Roger, Red Two, I'm on my way."

Raincloud came over the other radio, "Raincloud Flight, drop troops and exit east ASAP."

Bullets were slamming into my bird with thunderous bangs. The radios became a scrambled mess of words "Break off!", "Heavy fire!", "I've been hit!", "Lay down fire!" It was almost impossible to tell who was saying what.

I felt a sharp burning pain in my right leg just above the knee and knew that I had been hit by one of the projectiles being hurled at me from below. My aircraft was beginning to resemble Swiss cheese but I had nowhere to go. I could not continue to bank right as I would fly into the Raincloud Flight who was exiting the LZ, and if I banked back to the left I would fly right into the massive source of fire that was now filling my bird with holes. So continuing to fire my sixteen-pounders at the source of Red One's fire, I hoped to be able to cease their fire enough to overfly them and climb up after passing them.

Then came a tremendous bang and my master caution light began flashing "ENGINE" and the engine RPM went to zero. Bottoming the collective to preserve the rotor RPM and looking for somewhere to set down, I simultaneously broadcasted, "Red Two is going down to the north! May Day! May Day!"

Not being able to find a clearing to land in, I knew I would have to go into the trees. Maintaining my heading of north, which was into the wind, I tried to glide as far past the source of fire as possible, and then began to reduce my speed. At treetop level and with zero airspeed I began to pull up on the collective trying to settle into the trees as gently as I could and with the least amount of rotor RPM as possible. The tail rotor hit the trees first causing the wounded aircraft to lurch forward, then the main rotor hit, hurling the bird to one side and slamming it into the trees. As the aircraft came apart, everything went black.

13

CHAPTER 4

As consciousness began creeping back into my body, I felt this burning pain coming from my leg. I could also make out the sensation of movement about me and the muffled sounds of voices. My mind, however, wasn't making any sense. It was as if I were in a heavy fog, trying to wake up after a drunken stupor and trying to remember what I did and where I was awakening. The fog started to dissipate as my mind began to answer my questions by recounting the crash.

I snapped back to reality and realized that the scurrying bodies around me must be Vietcong. I reached for my forty-five that I always carried, but it was gone. Wait! I wasn't in the aircraft and everything had been removed from my pockets. A flash of fear sent shivers through my body as I tried to force my mind to give me some course of action.

I felt something poking me in the side and turned my head, trying to focus my eyes. There stood a young boy, that I would guess to be about sixteen years of age, dressed in some scroungy black pajamas and a pointed coolie hat. As he kept jamming the muzzle of his rifle into my side, I could see his mouth moving but the noise he made was just a slur.

Two more men scampered over and looked down at me. They were somewhat older, but dressed in the same scrungy garb as the boy. One of them began yelling at me in what was but a bunch of scrambled tones. When I did not respond, he picked up his foot and brought it down full force on my injured leg. The pain immediately sent waves of heat flashes through my entire body and I screamed out. Looking down at me with a sneer, he began to chuckle, taking great satisfaction that he could make me cry out with pain. The chuckle

14

soon faded and an intense look came to his face. He raised his rifle pointing the muzzle right at my head and the look in his eye told me there soon would be no more pain.

A voice rang out and the soldier's head came up off his aim and he relaxed the grip on the weapon pointing at my head. Turning his head toward the voice but keeping his rifle pointed somewhat at my head, he mumbled something in return. As the voice came into my field of vision it responded to the rifleman in a curt directive tone, and the rifle was then relaxed to the man's side.

I took a deep breath and exhaled slowly, in relief of what just about took place. My mind rationalized that this person with the life-saving voice must be in charge of this band of Vietcong. There was, however, nothing to distinguish him from the others except his mannerisms of being in charge.

As he looked down at me, he spoke in broken English. "You Officer GI?" I nodded my head in a positive response, believing that this would keep me alive and also keep me from being kicked again. If, however, I only knew what was to lie ahead for me, I might never have responded the way I did and hopefully received that fatal shot that the other man wanted to fire.

This person that seemed to be in charge then asked me in half-broken English but mostly in Vietnamese if I was part of the assault that had just taken place. I really didn't understand most of what he was saying, but from the few words of English that he did use and his gestures I thought that was pretty much the gist of what he asked. I wrinkled up my brows and shrugged my shoulders saying, "I don't understand."

As he stared at me with a blank look on his face, I wondered if he believed me or not. About then one of his subordinates came over and handed him my maps, charts, and flight bag. He took the items, peering at the section the map was folded to, and then again resumed his stare at me. In my mind I knew that he now had to know I was part of the assault from the markings on the map.

He again tried to question me, this time waving the maps and charts and once again I claimed that I could not understand what it was he was asking. Pressing his lips tight together he gave me an annoyed look and tried once more this time with more hand gestures.

15

With a real confused look on my face once more I claimed not to understand.

Turning to a small group of his men he mumbled more of his unintelligible language and two rushed to me. They motioned for me to get to my feet. I responded by shaking my head, telling them that I couldn't, and pointed to my leg. Apparently they were not concerned with my wound or my pain. They grabbed me by both arms and jerked me to my feet. The pain instantly sprang through my body and I cried out but did not fight against the action.

Once to my feet I realized that the bullet had passed completely through the fatty part of my thigh and didn't do any major damage to the bone or anything. I motioned to the one in charge, asking to be able to care for my leg and he nodded ok. I pointed to my handkerchief that was on the ground with the rest of my things they had taken from me, and he bent down then handed it to me. Ripping a hole in my flight suit, I discovered that the bleeding had already pretty much stopped. I wrapped the handkerchief around the wound and tied it real tight to keep it from bleeding further.

The two at my side motioned for me to walk in the direction that they were pointing. I pretended that my leg hurt worse than it really did and complained that I could not walk. The guard on my left shoved me in the direction they wanted me to go and I tumbled to the ground, landing at the feet of the one in charge. He looked down at me, and then mumbled more of his words to his troops. Two more, including the one that wanted to squeeze off a round to my head, joined the two already by my side. The one in charge then turned, walked over to where the main body of troops were gathered, and in a commanding voice mumbled more words to the four left behind with me. This was the last I was ever to see of the life-saving voice that condemned me to a living hell.

The one with an itchy trigger finger lashed out some indistinguishable commanding words and pointed with his head. I took these words to mean that we were going to move out in the opposite direction as the main body. By the way Itchy Finger looked at me I figured that I had better not give him any reason to administer any painful acts towards me. I climbed to my feet and tried not to put too much weight on my leg. The soldier behind me nudged me in the direction that Itchy Finger had pointed, and I stumbled forward, slowly limping in that direction.

The torrid hot afternoon was typical here. The sun's rays peeked through splotched holes in the canopy-like foliage overhead and the humidity engulfed the entire jungle like an invisible mist. The jungle, displaying its robe of green and with its background music of all the normal jungle noises, made it seem like a serene tropical paradise. However, the four armed guerilla warfare specialists that escorted me were a constant reminder that in reality there was a war going on.

As we walked I prayed that the assault was a success, which afforded me the hope of being rescued. I realized that we were going north or maybe northwest, in the opposite direction that the assault took place. Knowing the further north we got the slimmer my chances of rescue became, I tried to limp along as slowly as possible. After awhile the pain in my leg became a steady ache and I continuously tried to stop, asking to rest it. I did this not only because my leg really did hurt, but also as a stalling tactic. However the guard behind me wasn't concerned with my discomfort and would keep nudging me forward.

The light began to fade into the dusk of evening and hopefully we soon would stop for the night. My mind kept searching for some type of plan that would allow me to rid myself of my captors. As darkness began to surround us, the guards with their dark skin and black pajamas began to blend with the jungle. Now I could see why Charlie moved at night and my hope of stopping soon faded.

The path widened into a small clearing and the guard gestured to the spot where he wanted me to sit. As I sat there trying to care for my leg, the four guards squatted around me in their normal fashion with their butts almost dragging the ground and knees at about chin level. They reached into small canvas type bags they were carrying and pulled out little porcelain like bowls that in all probability had never been washed. Each promptly filled his bowl with rice that had to be at least a week old and began to shovel the substance into his mouth with his hands. One of the guards scooped a handful and held it out to me, the sight of which almost made me nauseous, and I shook my head no.

My mind continued to race, half the time calculating a way to free myself and half the time wondering where I was going and what was going to happen. Itchy Finger's mind was also hard at work, I guess. Never taking his eyes off me, he had the look of wanting me to do something that would allow him to scratch that itch in his finger.

CHAPTER 5

We walked for two more days, only stopping for three or four hours at a time to rest and allow the guards to ingest their, what I considered inedible, rice. Finally we arrived at what appeared to be a village. From a distance it seemed to be just a common village with numerous round straw and bamboo hooch's. As we neared the village I could see that the small hooch's surrounded a much larger square shaped hooch and had three more long rectangular hooch's off to one side. The village was encircled with barb wire barely visible through the elephant grass.

My blood ran cold with the realization that this was not just a village. The inhabitants here were not Vietnamese villagers nor were they Vietcong. They did not wear the wrap-around cloth garb of villagers or the black pajamas of the VC. They were clad in Khaki type uniforms. No, this was not a village, it was an NVA (North Vietnamese Army) outpost. However, as I soon would learn, it housed more than just the NVA.

One of the perimeter sentries stopped us at the entrance and Itchy Finger spoke to him in their native tongue. The sentry finally pointed to the large structure and we entered the gates of hell.

When we arrived in front of the large hooch, Itchy Finger left me with his cong counterparts and went inside. Ten to fifteen minutes later he returned, accompanied with two huskier than normal Vietnamese guards. These two goons, as they later became known, quickly swept me inside to a large room. The room was bare except for a sneering man peering at me from his desk. I was positioned in front of the desk and the goons took a couple of steps backwards, standing rigid at the position of attention.

My trip to hell was now complete, and here in front of me sat the devil himself. This would be the first of many, many painful interrogations that he would administer.

The room was about twenty feet square and had only one window in the opposite wall from the door. The desk was positioned under the window leaving the rest of the room barren. On the side of the desk was an oil burning lamp that looked like it belonged in an antique shop somewhere. My flight bag, maps, and charts taken from the aircraft lay on the desk.

The man behind the desk stood up clutching my dog tags in his hand and walked to the side of the desk, then cleared a corner and sat there. My stomach churned itself into a knot and my mind ran rampant.

The silence was finally broken, "I am told that you are a pilot, is that correct?"

As I nodded my head yes I was in complete amazement that this oriental in his mid-thirties could speak almost perfect English.

"Are these your dog tags?" he asked with a sadistic smile creeping across his face.

I shrugged my shoulders.

He stood up, laying the dog tags on the desk and pointed to my leg. "Is your leg hurt bad and require medical attention?"

I answered that I would like a doctor to look at it.

"As soon as you help me here with a few questions that I have I will see to it that you are well cared for."

What kind of questions, I wondered. I didn't really know anything that would aid them. Then my mind went back to classes I was required to attend years ago on the code of conduct. All I was required to give was my name, rank and service number, and nothing that would aid the enemy.

"Now according to your maps here...," he paused and looked up at me, "These are your maps, aren't they?"

"My name is John Walker, I am a first lieutenant in the United States Army and my service number is 01731157."

He gave out a half-chuckle, shook his head and with a 'how dumb are you' look, said, "Yes, lieutenant, I know all that, but I wish to know about the markings on your map here."

"According to the Geneva Convention I am only required to give you my name, rank and service number."

"Now now, lieutenant, we are friends here, and all I am asking is what we really already know. You see lieutenant, the Americans have committed a great wrong against the Peoples' Republic of Vietnam and all we ask is that you admit to the wrongs you have committed against us and show that you are truly sorry and wish our forgiveness. You will find that we are a very forgiving people, lieutenant. You will see our goodness and be well cared for if you confess your wrongs."

What was he asking me to do here? "What wrongs against you have we committed?" I asked.

He went on to say that the imperialist American Government had killed many innocent women and children and tried to turn the people against their government with lies. That the whole war was caused by the Americans and that it was time that they admitted their wrongdoings to the world. "I understand that as a soldier you were following orders and committed these wrongdoings because your superiors have told you to do so. However you, like the others here, will realize that the American Government is the demon and we are the victims. You must confess your actions, seek forgiveness and begin to right your wrongs. Surely, lieutenant, you can see that your government does not care what happens to you."

I could not believe my ears. Here this man was asking me, or worse yet telling me, that I had to confess to evil acts that I had not done nor had my country done. I became so enraged at what I was asked to do that I blurted out, "You're full of shit! My name is John Walker, I am a first lieutenant and my service number is 01731157, and under the Geneva Convention as a prisoner of war that is all I am required to say." When I heard those words come from my mouth it sent chills down my spine. I was just now accepting the realization of that was what I was. A POW.

His snide little smile instantly fell into a stern scowl. "Now lieutenant," his voice now intense rather than relaxed as before, "first of all, the Peoples' Republic of Vietnam is not a signatory of the Geneva Convention and second, you are not a prisoner of war. You are an American spy, and as a spy you will be tried and shot unless you cooperate. Now lieutenant," his voice became relaxed again as he continued, "I want to be your friend, don't make this hard on both of us."

I was totally unprepared for what I was hearing. I truly believed in what my country was doing in Vietnam and the causes that we were fighting for. This was one of the hardest wars to fight that my country had ever been in, and although I sometimes did not agree with the way we were fighting it, I did believe in my country.

I thought it ludicrous that this man, a representative of an inhumane dictatorship, be telling me about the wrongdoings that I and my country have committed. I knew first hand of the atrocities committed by this barbaric government and the complete disregard for human life that they had. Then he has the nerve to call me not only an evildoer but a spy. "You know that I'm no spy. You're fucking crazy!"

No sooner had the words left my mouth when I received a kick from one of his goons behind me, landing purposefully on my wounded leg. A streak of lighting rushed through my body as I fell to the floor. Suddenly the other goon's foot was planted full force into my chest, taking every bit of breath I had away.

As I lay there gasping for air his sadistic smile returned to his face and he said, "The first lesson you must learn, lieutenant, is the proper respect for me and the Peoples' Republic of Vietnam. Now lieutenant, the guards will take you to your new home and I am going to give you some time to think about what I have told you. I hope that on our next meeting you will have more respect and be more cooperative." Returning to his mother tongue he gave orders to his two goons.

Quickly the goons swooped down grabbing me by the arms. With the pain in my leg throbbing and still gasping for precious air, I was dragged to one of the smaller hooch's. The already small hooch was divided into even smaller cages separated by a bamboo type curtain, and each was no bigger than a six foot by ten foot closet.

They opened the cage door and shoved me inside to the floor then followed me in. One jerked me to my feet as the other slammed his fist into my face then the midsection, collapsing me once again to the floor. They took turns picking me up and practicing their karate on me, and neither needed practice. After what seemed like an eternity and one or two final kicks, they left me in a quivering and bleeding pile of flesh, still coughing and gasping for life-supporting air.

After lying there close to unconsciousness for about an hour my breath began to return. I pulled myself to the wall and sat up against it, wiping the blood from my face with my sleeve. Wondering if anyone else was caged here, in a breathless voice I spoke, "Is—is there—any other—American—in here?"

As I waited for an answer I heard scrambling then my door opened and here were the goons again. One yelled to me in very broken English, "No talkie!" followed with a few more kicks to the head and body.

Again I found myself trying to regain my senses, and upright myself to a sitting position against the wall. Although I thought it was still daylight outside I was unable to see much light. I raised my hand to my face and discovered two lumps about the size of golf balls in place of my eyes. Wondering what my face looked like, I continued to feel it but couldn't tell much other than my nose was still bleeding. At this point I could not tell what part of my body ached more.

My mind began to rummage through everything that had happened. What was I suppose to do now? I knew that it was my duty as an officer to try to escape, but how?

I started to feel around the cage because my eyes would not allow images in. It felt as if it were constructed of bamboo bars and covered with straw of some kind. It shouldn't be that hard to break through, but I was too weak at this point. I told myself that it would be best to rest awhile and try to regain my strength and sight.

I rolled away from the wall and half curled up on my side to get some rest but my mind continued to race. I lay there thinking of different ways to escape but each plan would be scrapped due to my lack of sight or mobility. My mind sorted through hundreds of plans but each was impractical. My thoughts were beginning to run together and nothing was making sense. I tried to clear my head and rest, hoping I could think more clearly later. Not having much sleep for the last few days was beginning to take its toll and I began to drift off.

It seemed that I had just entered slumber land when I heard the door open. I tried to open my eyes to see but could only manage two little slits and was unable to distinguish anything but shadows. Someone grabbed me by the arms and I presumed it to be the two goons who used me as a practicing dummy. They jerked me to my feet and pulled me to the door. Unable to navigate myself they held a tight grip on my arms and roughly directed me out of the hooch.

My mind quickly began to try and unscramble itself. I figured that I was being taken back to the English speaking officer and I tried to think of what I should do and say. I decided that no matter what I would not confess to anything nor would I betray my country.

As we reached the empty room I realized that it must be dark outside because in here I could see the faint flickering light from the lamp I had seen earlier. I could also make out the blurred figure of a person sitting behind the desk as the two goons jerked me to a stop in front of it. The blurred image behind the desk stood up and walked to the side of the desk as he had done before. Only this time instead of sitting on the corner he just folded his arms and said, "Well now lieutenant, I presume that you have learned the lesson of respect".

My stomach was churning itself in knots and my body trembling from the sound of his voice. I nodded my head in a positive response.

"Good," he was now trying to talk in a friendly tone as he walked back around the desk and took his seat. "Now let's resume our little talk and you can answer a few questions for me. These are your maps, now, aren't they?"

My fear ran rampant through my body and I could not stop trembling. I flexed the muscles of my body and stiffened to a form that resembled the position of attention. This would aid me in mustering up the courage to carry out my decision to tell him nothing. "My name is John Walker, my rank is first lieutenant—."

I barely got out the word lieutenant when one of the goons rammed the butt of his rifle into my midsection forcing all the air from my lungs and sending me to my knees. They quickly jerked me to my feet as I again was gasping for air.

"Now lieutenant, surely you can see that this whole thing is going to be much easier if you cooperate. You are not betraying your country by answering my questions. Most of your fellow countrymen have already put down the actions of your government and it is your government who has betrayed you. You can see that, can't you?"

As I stood there half hunched over trying to regain the ability to suck in air, I told myself I had to be strong and not answer his questions. I raised my head and tried to glare at him through my almost swollen shut eyes.

In an almost exasperated voice he asked, "Now lieutenant, is this your map?"

I got as far as "My name is A—." This time the rifle butt found my face, snapping my head back and hurling me backwards to the floor. Again the goons immediately jerked me back to my feet. My head was spinning and my legs felt as though they would give way at any minute. I could feel the warm blood running from my nose once again.

How much more of this would they do? How much more could I take?

This treatment went on for what seemed like forever but in reality it was only about an hour. I was becoming incoherent and unable to make sense of anything. I could barely stand on my feet and would waver and fall to the floor, being quickly and roughly erected by the goons.

Finally the question came again, "Is this your map?" and I weakly nodded my head yes.

"Now see, lieutenant," there was now a self satisfaction in his voice, "that wasn't so hard, was it?" I shook my limp head no.

It didn't make sense to continue this punishment since the answers to his questions he already had. The mission had taken place, what, three, four or was it five days ago. Besides I didn't have the strength to take anymore.

He continued asking me questions about the mission. How many troops were inserted? What base did they come from? What was their mission? And so on. I answered the questions in a mumbled slur that I really don't think he could make sense of, and things I didn't really know I lied about. Nonetheless, whatever answer I gave seemed to satisfy him. The main thing to me was that the rifle butts were not taking a toll on my already broken and bloody body anymore.

After answering his questions for what seemed an endless period of time he said, "All right lieutenant, you seem tired. You have done well and you shall see that this is the best way. You go get some rest now and we will talk again later."

The two goons took me by the arms, this time not so roughly, and escorted me back to the cage that I was put in earlier. Once there, I laid down on the floor and whether it was that I was so tired or I just passed out from the pain of the savage beating, I don't know. Whichever it was, I quickly fell into a deep sleep that I needed so desperately.

CHAPTER 6

I awoke to the sound of my cage door opening and a rustling noise. "Oh God, not another talk, not now," I pleaded silently. I knew that I did not have the strength or the energy to combat their savage tactics to extract undeserving confessions. Then the sound of the door closing and footsteps leaving allowed me to sigh in relief.

I tried to open my eyes but the swelling would only allow light to appear through two small slits. Straining my eyes to focus, I could make out two small objects left inside the cage by the door, but could not tell what they were. When I attempted to move, my entire body was engulfed in pain. Their methodical savagery had left no part of my being unbattered. My abdominal muscles were so tender it was impossible to sit up and even hurt terribly just to fill my lungs with air. My head throbbed worse than any headache I had ever had, or could imagine having, and the slightest movement sent waves of thunder clamoring throughout.

I rolled over onto my stomach, wincing from the massive pain my body was feeling. Pulling myself the few feet to the front of the cage I braced my broken body against the wall, and stared down at the objects left there on the floor. One was a small porcelain bowl of rice about the size of a coffee cup. The white rice was seeded throughout with black and brown objects, the sight of which was disgusting and left me with no desire to eat it. The second object was a can about the size of a tomato juice can, filled with a murky water. My mouth and throat were so dry and gritty that regardless of the dirtiness of the water, it looked inviting.

I reached down and picked up the can of water, pulling it to my mouth. I sucked the beautiful off-colored water through my swollen and cut lips and swallowed. Even though it hurt to just swallow, I don't remember water ever tasting so good. Pouring some into my hand, I splashed it over my face and head, and the coolness eased some of the throbbing. I raised the can back to my lips and quickly drank the rest. When the can was empty instead of expending the energy to set it back down, I just let it fall, clanging to the floor. I then lay back down and slipped into an unconscious state once again.

How long I was out this time I don't know but when I came to, there was another can of water and either a new bowl of rice or the same one that was left earlier. I pulled myself to a sitting position against the wall and was amazed at the tremendous amount of energy needed to do so. Never before had I experienced such an intense pain that encompassed my body so totally. Little did I know that the pain could and would get worse.

I reached down grasping the can of water with both hands and took a long drink, allowing the liquid to slide down my throat. Holding the tin in my lap I dipped my hand into it and wiped the coolness across my bulging eyes. As I sat there with my head braced to the wall, the pangs of hunger growled from inside. I began to think, when was it I last ate, five days ago or was it six? Pulling my head forward I looked down at the bowl of rice. No longer did the black and brown objects mixed in with the white kernels look disgusting. I sat the can of water down and picked up the bowl of rice, raising it to my nose to get a smell. My nose, however, was so full of dried blood it was impossible to suck any air through it. I scooped a handful from the bowl and stuffed it into my mouth. I can't remember it even having a taste but quickly ate the entire small portion. After setting down the empty bowl I picked up the can of water, sprinkled more across my face then drank the rest. The skimpy portion of rice served as a teasing appetizer and my stomach cried out for more. I knew, however, that was all I would receive for awhile.

I rested my head back on the wall and let my subconscious drift. Images of my high school days rose to life. I was a standout athlete back then, but my recollections were not of my best sport, baseball, they were of football. I recalled complaining about the rigorous exercises that the merciless coaches would put us through. I would awaken stiff and sore and moan all day because of my achy muscles, then be right back out on the field that afternoon going through all the drills. No one would let on to the coach, however, that they were sore or even tired because that would bring on more repetitions to whip us into shape. There were days that I thought my body could take no more and I was at my end but still kept going. When the coach would finally say, "Hit the showers," I always felt good about myself for not giving in or quitting. I hoped that the stamina taught to me then would stay with me now and help me get through the anguish and torture yet to come.

The evening sun had already slipped away and the coolness that the darkness brought felt good. I told myself how nice it would be if I could just feel some kind of breeze. Although the outside opening to the hooch had no door, the cage was completely enclosed and allowed no air to circulate.

As I sat there enjoying the coolness of the night I thought how good it would feel to take a shower. I hadn't had one in about a week now. My hair was matted with dried blood and my skin sticky from sweat. My flight suit was tattered and torn and reeked of body odor.

I laid my weary body down and drifted off, dreaming of home, shower, and the feeling of crawling into a nice soft bed with clean sheets.

Once again I awoke the next morning to the sound of my door opening. I tensed my body and prayed. Maybe I was being overly jumpy but the thought of the goons coming to take me for another little talk sent tense tingling senses of terror through my nervous system.

My fear was for naught, however; it was one of the guards bringing me my morning ration. In addition to my undersized bowl of rice and tin of murky water he brought two other items. The first item, which he sat off to one side, was a bucket that, I deduced from his broken language and gestures, was to be used for human waste. The other item was a medium sized metal wash basin filled with the same cloudy water as in my drinking tin.

After the gift-bearing guard exited, I pulled myself up to a sitting position. I noticed that the throbbing had somewhat subsided, but I was still extremely tender and sore, making movement difficult. Scooting over to my ration, I picked up the puny bowl of rice and shoveled it into my mouth, then drank half my tin of water.

Setting down the tin, I sat back and began to unlace my boots. This was the first time, since my capture, that I had removed them.

Then, using the wall as a crutch, I rose to my feet very gingerly. I was dizzy, weak, and very sore, but managed to unzip my flight suit, pulling it off over my shoulders and letting it fall to the floor around my ankles. Sliding back down the wall to a sitting position, I pulled the basin over between my legs. I first untied the handkerchief from my punctured leg and rinsed it out. Then, using the cloth as a washrag, I began to cleanse my body, washing away the dried blood and other dinginess. Once that was completed, I submerged my flight suit in the now brownish colored water of the basin. After rinsing it the best I could, I rang all the water out possible and laid it out on the floor to dry. Feeling somewhat clean and a hundred times better, I laid my head back against the wall to relax and to think.

I knew as I sat there that I could not allow my mind to become nonfunctional and drift from thought to thought. Even though a certain amount of drifting back in time and dreaming was necessary to keep my hope alive, it was also important to force my brain to make judgments and reasonings to maintain its functions. If I didn't force the exercise of my brain it may slip into a valley of despair and be useless when the time came to escape. One of the first assignments that I taxed my brain with was to calculate how long I had been here.

Upon completion of pondering back and dividing the period of time into days I settled on eight days that had elapsed since my capture. Since I had no calendar and my watch, which kept the date, had been taken from me when I was captured I had to devise a way to keep track of time. The outer wall was made of a straw-like grass so I pulled several reeds from it and broke them into eight pieces; then I placed the pieces between the bamboo slats on the outside wall. At the end of each day I would add one more reed.

In addition to keeping my mental state up I also knew that I must keep my physical condition up. My body was in no condition, however, for rigorous exercises, but light walking would do me some good. I pulled myself to my feet and holding on to the wall began to walk the length of my cage, about four steps each way. My muscles cried out from the soreness and after several trips I vowed to do more tomorrow.

Soon the guard was there again bringing me my measly portion of rice and refilling my water tin. This time rather than gulping down the rice I ate it slowly. I would put only a few kernels in my mouth at a time and drink some water between each portion. I thought that this tactic would trick my stomach into believing that I had eaten more than I really had, but it didn't work. I was still hungry.

The coolness of night began to fill the air and the light was fading. I reached for my flight suit to see if it was dry and it was. Exerting a great amount of effort, I pulled the suit and my boots back on. I then sat there and thought how quickly the day had passed, and wondered how many more I would have to go through.

Over the next few days I came down with what I at first thought to be malaria, but realized it was my body rejecting the unsanitary conditions. Between the fever, vomiting, and diarrhea I became very weak and dehydrated. I figured that if I forced myself to keep eating and drinking my body would adjust and I was right. Slowly the symptoms went away and I resumed my mental and physical exercises.

About four weeks went by without any contact with the outside world except for the brief moments the guards would bring my rations. They would come twice a day, in the mornings they would fill my rice bowl, water tin, and the wash basin; then in the evening just the bowl and tin. Every two or three days they would make an extra trip to empty my waste bucket. There were never any words spoken by either of us as they went about their chores. When they came they never went to any of the other cages in this hooch, so I assumed that I was the only one here. However, usually late in the afternoon, sometimes I would hear anguishing screams of pain which meant there were other Americans in the compound. I often would ponder on how many were here and where they were caged, and wished I could talk to them.

My mind was always occupied with trying to escape. I managed to make a small hole in the outer wall and see that there were two guards watching each hooch at all times. I also remembered that the camp was surrounded with barb wire and wondered if there were mines there too. The long hooch's at the end of the compound that I observed when I arrived were probably troop quarters and could house thirty to fifty people. I stored all this information away as it seemed the chances of escape were unlikely with such limited facts, but I could use the knowledge later.

31

Jerry Wood

As I sat one afternoon, counting the bamboo slats in the wall, I heard footsteps coming to my hooch. I thought it odd that the guards would be coming around this early. When the door opened a rain of terror flashed through my mind and my body tensed. Standing there were the goons motioning for me to come out. I began to tremble as I tried to rise to my feet. My legs were quivering so, it was hard for them to support my weight. My mind began to plead, "Oh God no, please no!"

CHAPTER 7

I was once again taken to the large square hooch and into the room where the English speaking officer sat behind the lone desk. I was positioned in front of the desk and the goons took their positions behind me, like always he stood and walked to the corner and sat.

"How are you today lieutenant?" he asked as he lit up a cigarette.

I replied that I was fine.

He held out the pack of cigarettes, "Cigarette, lieutenant?"

I hadn't had one since I was shot down and his expelled smoke made me yearn for one. After wrestling with whether I should or should not accept one, I finally nodded yes and he lit it for me.

As I took a long drag that sent a mild rush to my head, he continued in his friendly voice but yet smirky tone, "I presume you are being well cared for".

I didn't think that this was the time to complain and said that I was.

"Good, good. Now lieutenant," he had a habit of always starting his thoughts with the word 'now', "I wanted to have a little talk with you earlier, but unfortunately I have been very busy. I would like for us to get to know each other better and this way you can see that what I have told you is true about us. So now lieutenant, tell me about yourself."

I didn't know what to tell him because I didn't want to give him anything he could use. However I didn't want the butt end of the rifles again, either. "What do you want to know?" I asked.

He chuckled, walking back around his desk and sitting down. "Are you married? Do you have children? Where are you from? You know, things like that."

Children! The word ran through my head. My wife was expecting our second child when I was captured. I wondered if she had it yet and what it was. God, I wished I was there.

"Yes I'm married and have one son," I answered, thinking it wouldn't hurt to answer these questions but decided not to tell him about my wife expecting another.

"I bet you really miss them, don't you?"

I replied that I did as I tried to figure out the point of all this.

"I understand you missing them. You see, I too have a wife and son. They are in Hanoi. Tell me lieutenant, how long has it been since you last saw them?"

I couldn't understand the reason for these questions. I didn't believe he brought me in here just to get to know me. What was he after?

"It's been about eight months."

"That long. Perhaps you would like to write them a letter. Would you like that?"

Again I was confused as to the point. I didn't know how to answer or what answer he wanted. I nodded my head yes.

"I will arrange it. Here, I want you to see this." Standing up, he held out a wrinkled newspaper clipping. I took the scrap and scanned the article. It was about some Vietnam protesters in the United States. "You see lieutenant, as I told you, even your countrymen recognize the wrongs your Government has committed against us. Look at this." He took the article back and shoved a piece of paper across his desk to me. "This is a confession by one of your comrades here, where he tells of the deeds he has done at the orders of his commanders".

I didn't know how to respond. I knew that he probably got the confession by beating the person into submission, but what did he want from me? Was he now going to want a confession from me? I still didn't know his purpose for all this, so I just stood there.

He handed me a blank piece of paper and a short pencil, "Here lieutenant, take this and write a nice letter to your wife and son. We will talk some more tomorrow. Bring your letter with you and I will see that it is sent for you."

With his snide little smile he sat down in his chair and rattled off some garble to his goons. They took me by the arms and escorted me back to my cage.

I sat in total confusion. Why would he want me to write a letter home? Why did he show me that article and confession? I didn't know what his purpose was but knew there was something to be gained by him in this.

Not being able to see where a letter to my wife would benefit him in any way but may help my family, I chose to write a short note. I decided, however, that I didn't want to give him my address so I would address it to the United States Army to be forwarded to my wife. With those decisions made, I asked myself, "What do I write?" I couldn't tell her where I was; I didn't know myself. I didn't want to upset her so I couldn't write about my treatment.

After pondering what to put in the letter I finally began to write. "My dearest darling," followed by about five lines of hoping the letter found them all well, I loved them and not to worry, then signed "All my love, John." Considering that I hadn't seen my family in so long, it was an awfully short letter, but in this set of circumstances it would have to suffice.

Not much later the guard came around with my ration. I ate the sparse meal then lay back with the letter in my hand. I began to wonder if my wife had already had the baby and what it was. I wondered how big my son must be by now and hoped they all were well. My wife was staying with her mother and I knew that she would help her through this. I was sure that the Army would continue to send her my pay, so money would not be a worry. I continued to think of them till I drifted off to sleep.

The next afternoon the two goons were at my door again. They took me to the empty room where, as always, the English speaking officer would stand and walk to the edge of his desk.

"Good afternoon lieutenant. How are you today?"

"Fine," I responded.

"Good. I see you have brought your letter, let me see it." Taking it from my hand, he looked at the few lines that I had written and shook his head. "Now lieutenant, this will not do at all. They are going to want to know more. Here let me help you, I am very good at letters." Handing me back the paper, he began to dictate, "Tell them

35

that you are being well cared for and that you have realized the wrongs that your government is committing against the Peoples' Republic of Vietnam." He stopped and with a stern tone said, "Lieutenant, you are not writing."

Everything was starting to make sense now. He wanted a letter not to my family, but a propaganda letter. I told myself that I could not write a letter like that and let it be used to embarrass my Government.

I half flipped the letter I had written earlier to his desk and said, "Neither I nor my country have committed any wrongs toward you or your government".

"Now lieutenant, I thought that we have come to an understanding. You know, I have successfully kept you from being tried as a spy but I need your cooperation. Surely you realize that I am your friend, don't you?"

"My name is John Walker, first lieutenant, my service number is 01731157."

Once again I found a rifle butt being rammed into my midsection, taking my breath away. I went to my knees and once again the goons jerked me back to my feet.

"Now lieutenant," his jaw was tensed and his voice demanding. "You will write this letter just as I tell you or I will have you shot as a spy. Do you understand?"

Unable to catch my breath I shook my head no, indicating that I would not write the letter. Again the rifle butt found my midsection, knocking me to my knees gasping for air.

This time, however, instead of jerking me to my feet one of the goons pulled my arms behind me and the other wrapped a leather strap around my upper arms. They cinched the strap pulling my arms together behind me. The pain was excruciating and I cried out.

"Now lieutenant," changing to his sadistic tone, "it will be much easier on you if you write the letter."

Again I shook my head no and caught the rifle butt full force in my face. The force of the blow knocked me backwards onto my tied arms and I screamed out in pain.

After a lengthy bout with the rifle butts, my face once again was rearranged into a bloody mess and my chest felt as if it would explode at any second. Barely coherent, I finally agreed to write the letter.

The goons removed the strap and jerked me to the desk. The officer put a pencil in my hand and began to dictate. My hands were numb and I couldn't feel the pencil at all. However I managed to scratch out what he told me to. It was almost completely illegible and had the look of a child's writing for the first time. Once again, however, it seemed to satisfy the fiend, and the two goons returned me to my cage and left me on the floor, suffering and moaning.

CHAPTER 8

I found myself once more awakening to a massive amount of pain that, before this, I would never believe the human body could possibly endure. My arms had pulsating waves of sharp pain surging through them, but were numb to the touch. I had to labor to even bring air to my lungs as my chest was still on fire. The pounding in my head was so severe that it almost in itself immobilized me.

Tears began to fill my battered eyes, but not from the agonizing pain of my body. Yes, they inflicted more hurt and pain this time, but they did more than just brutalize my body. This time they injured my self-respect and my pride. Maybe not in a big way, but nonetheless I had betrayed my country and that hurt was as real as the hurt that screamed throughout my body. I gave the enemy one more bullet to use in their propaganda campaign. I wondered what they would want next time and what they would do to get it. I told myself that no matter what they would do to me the next time, I would have to be strong and give them nothing further to use against not only my country but against others in the same position as myself.

When the guard brought my morning diet, I rolled over and with great effort crawled to the sparse chow. Since there was no feeling in my hands or fingers I had to be very careful not to spill the limited ration. After consuming my meal I tugged at the newly filled basin, bringing it close to me and began to splash the liquid to my face and head. The water soon changed from its cloudy state to a rusty brown from the dried blood that now covered my body. I knew that I needed to bathe my entire body, but all my strength had been siphoned out.

I sat there unable to even roll over to lie on the floor. Resting my heavy head back against the wall, I began to think about the letter. What would they do with it? My mind drifted to the thought of how I might be judged later for giving in. Surely anyone could tell that it wasn't written of my own free will, couldn't they? I wondered if the leaders of our great nation had anticipated or knew of the brutalities that I, and probably many other POWs, were experiencing here. Furthermore I wondered if they even cared, did anyone care?

I could feel myself slipping into despair and wallowing in self-pity. I told myself that doing this would not be good for me; it would only make me weaker and I needed to be strong. But right now I didn't care, crying myself quietly off to sleep.

After a couple days of commiseration for myself, and moping like a whipped pup, I bathed some of the filth from my body. The aches and pains had begun to ease, but I was still extremely tender. Pulling my flight suit, which now was resembling a moth eaten rag, from my person, I semi washed it out and laid it on the floor to dry. Now it was time to get my mental state back into shape.

I gathered my straws of time from the wall and began to count. There were sixty-four. I calculated that I had not added any for four days and quickly did so. This now brought my total to sixty-eight and carefully I replaced them in the wall.

Over the next several weeks I continued my exercises every day, building what limited strength I could. Based on the way my flight suit sagged around me, I figured that I had lost between forty to fifty pounds.

During those weeks of solitude I also learned to turn a dream into a movie show. I found that any time I chose I could escape into a world of fantasy. Sitting with my eyes closed I would concentrate on whatever scene I wanted and my subconscious would become a projector and play whatever show I wanted. The only problem with this was that I always had to return to reality, so to keep my mind alert I kept up with my other mental exercises too.

One afternoon I heard footsteps coming into my hooch. I knew that it wasn't time for my afternoon feeding and instant panic seized my being. My fears were eased somewhat when the door opened and the two standing there were not the husky goons of Satan. However they had no rations, and my mind frantically searched for explanations for their presence.

They curtly motioned for me to collect my things: bowl, can, basin, and bucket, and then step out. Placing the bowl and can inside inkih

the basin and holding that in one hand, I picked up the bucket and complied with their orders. As we marched to the other side of the compound again, my fears were eased a little when we did not stop at the large hooch. My mind raced through the possibilities of this action and found no answers as we stopped at another small hooch and I was deposited into a cage similar to the one I had just left.

As I sat my things down I wished I could have grabbed my straws of time. I told myself that wasn't a problem because I could remember the number: the count was one hundred and nineteen. Immediately I set out to start a new collection.

About half way through my count I heard rustling noises coming from the other cages. I concluded that there must be other Americans caged in this hooch and a great excitement came over me. At the mere thought of being able to talk with one of my own, an anticipation likened only to that of a small child on Christmas morning overwhelmed me. My mind was quick to remember the last time that I had cried out to talk to another, but I had to take the chance.

I knelt down close to the wall separating my cage from the next and whispered, "Is anyone over there?" After a moment a low reply came back to me, "Yes, but we can't talk now. Tonight." Then silence filled the air once more.

I could hardly wait for night to come.

CHAPTER 9

As the evening twilight began to set in, the guards arrived with my meager portion of rice and water. Unlike their trips to the other hooch, this time I could hear them stop at each cage leaving each prisoner his minute allotment of rice. Hearing these sounds made me even more aware of others being housed in this hooch.

I sat eating my morsels of rice and wondered when it would be safe to communicate. My entire being overflowed with eagerness at the opportunity to reestablish some type of link with humankind. I knew, however, that I could not jeopardize anyone by initiating the conversation. They would know when it was safe.

Darkness came, and I anxiously awaited for words to be spoken, but there were none. The only sounds were those of a rhythmic tapping, breaking the silence of the night. I had heard these noises before and disregarded them, but this time they were coming from within the hooch. I immediately thought: they're communicating in morse code. Why hadn't I thought of that before? I listened intently, trying to pick up the sequence of taps and was discouraged to realize that it wasn't morse code. It had to be some type of code, but what?

Suddenly the tapping stopped and a whisper came through the wall, "What's your name?"

"John. What's yours?" I replied in the same low whisper.

"Alan," he answered, and quickly went on to say it was against the rules to talk with each other and if caught we would be beaten. He continued by saying we could communicate by using the tapping code I had heard earlier, but never when the guards were nearby. Giving me the code, he told me to memorize it and that we would talk again later.

The tapping began once again between the cages. The code seemed to be a relatively simple one, so I tried to decipher what was being said. After a few minutes of frustration at not being able to keep up enough to make any sense of their unspoken conversation I dejectedly gave up. Soon the tapping words fell silent and I presumed that the others all fell asleep.

It took me several days to become familiar enough with this new way of conversing to really communicate effectively, and even longer to do it by reflex. The code itself was pretty simple, but in order to send an entire thought in a short message words and even sentences had to be abbreviated. These abbreviations were what made it so difficult to decipher a message, because you had to put your mind on the same wave-length as the sender.

During my first few weeks in my new dungeon I began to learn a little about my fellow captives, and of course told them of me. I learned that everyone else had given in to our captors under the agonizing acts of torture as I had done. Everyone that is except one, the man in the cage next to mine, the one who spoke to me the first night. Alan had withstood all forms of their merciless beatings and painful tortures and refused them everything. He said that he would put himself in a trance-like state which allowed him to withstand the massive amounts of pain inflicted. He admitted, however, that the days following an interrogation were very painful. In the months to come I would communicate with Alan at every opportunity and acquire the strength to survive from him.

Alan had been captured about a month prior to me while on a LIRP (Listening, Intelligence, and Reconnaissance Patrol) assignment. His squad of six men were gathering intelligence in the Ashau Valley on, as it turned out, the assault in which I was shot down. The team was discovered in the midst of night by a company of guerrillas outnumbering them by about five to one. The decision to surrender was made by Alan, as the team leader, and it haunted him every day. It seems that after they laid down their arms the VC shot three of his men right there in front of his eyes for no reason. The others, Brett and Randy, were there in the same hooch with us. Alan said he wished that he would have decided to fight rather than surrender, affording them the opportunity to die with dignity. I could tell that the decision caused him great internal pain, pain that he would bear the rest of his life even though he shouldn't have to.

Alan always kept my hope of escaping alive. We would continuously exchange information we had learned about the compound, guards, where we were, any little tidbit we could pick up. Most of the time this information was of very little importance and even useless but you never knew what might turn out to be a key.

Escape plans were solicited from everyone every day. There again all the plans were scrapped because of their impracticality or lack of means to carry them out. All this planning served a good purpose, however. It not only helped pass time, but it kept our minds alert and functioning plus it kept our morale up in the midst of turmoil and despair.

Whenever someone would be returned from interrogations and dumped into his cage in a mass of bloody flesh and bones, everyone became depressed and melancholy. Alan and I would quickly get everyone working on a new plan to escape, busying their minds. We must have gone through a million escape plans.

Alan and I became very close and always talked of things we would do when we got out. Alan was married and had two children, a boy and a girl. We would plan to get our families together for outings, knowing our wives would hit it off. These outings would include all kinds of extravagant things in extravagant places, like Europe, Hawaii, and the Bahamas to name just a few. We would spend hours talking about our families and how great our planned get-togethers would be. Sometimes everyone would join in and we'd plan a reunion with all of us and our families. Brett once asked if we had to invite Captain Now (the English speaking interrogator) and the goons to our reunion, too.

CHAPTER 10

As I sat one afternoon counting my straws of time, which I didn't need to do to know the count, I heard footsteps enter the hooch. With my count now up to two hundred and seventy-one, I knew the normal routine of the guards and the sound of these footsteps in the afternoon. I, as I'm sure all encaged did, froze and fear tensed my body. Who were they coming for? Please God, not me.

The sound of a cage door opening sent a sigh of relief that soon turned to sorrow. Someone was on his way to the painful room of Captain Now. Oh God, why does anyone have to endure this, I asked.

Upon the exit of the footsteps a quick roll was taken. Each of us would tap out our initials to signify our presence. This time it was Frank.

Frank was from Wisconsin, where he grew up on a dairy farm. He wasn't married, but often told us of his dream to return home and marry his childhood sweetheart. He entered the service before he graduated from college, believing that it was every young man's responsibility to serve his country. Frank was more of the nice down-home boy rather than the soldier type, however.

The last year of imprisonment was taking its toll on Frank. We noticed that in the last few months he was beginning to break mentally as well as physically. He wasn't exercising at all any more and rarely communicated. He was being taken for interrogation more and more, but coming back with less punishment and sat in his cage and sobbed for hours and hours. Sometimes we would try to out and out talk to him rather than tap, but he would not respond. Everyone was really concerned for Frank. We were also concerned for ourselves, as in his condition we didn't know what he might tell them.

44

After ten to fifteen minutes of silence we began to hear the sounds of his painful beating, sounds that we all knew so well. The thuds of the rifle butts and the shriek of his voice sent chills through our bodies and we could feel the pain of every blow. Later the screams ceased, but not the echoing thuds that crashed into his body. With tears in our eyes, we all wished that he would break and tell them what they wanted to know. As we later learned, they wanted Frank to give them the code of our communications. This time Frank never broke; he also never returned to his cage.

Our captors were always frustrated at their inability to break our code. Its simplicity and the fact that everything had to be abbreviated kept them from ever catching on. Many of us took very severe beatings, but that was the one thing that no one would give in on. The code was what gave us some resemblance of a group and was the cement that held our hopes and plans together. Without it we would be totally isolated and lost on our own, but with it we drew on the strength of the group. The code became sacred. Even to this day I have it etched deep in my mind, but hesitate ever to give it out. Even Frank, who was totally broken, died before giving up the code.

After Frank's death, the interrogations came to a stop for about a month. Up to this point, for some the interrogations were becoming less severe and more frequent, which meant that they were giving in to the barbarians without much inducement. Although we almost never had the opportunity to see any other POWs, we were able to keep close tabs on each other's conditions. Alan and I continuously worked at keeping everyone's spirit up by getting all to think about helping each other rather than wallowing in self pity, but we were beginning to think our efforts were failing.

The stoppage of beatings saved us from being thrust into despair. It gave us the opportunity to rejuvenate ourselves and pick up our spirits with more hope than ever. We set out on a mission to collect every bit of information we could, and everyone was contributing to our plans of escape. During this time, everyone started to believe that the war would soon be over or that we would be able to escape, either of which would put us in the heaven of freedom. Although our meager daily allotment of nourishment was far below that of even poverty level, our bodies began to heal and this along with our intense planning campaign made us mentally stronger too. I don't think anyone can forget the savage brutalities we were forced to endure, but for that short time we were able to set aside the fears of the next beating and not let it occupy our thoughts.

The heads of the POW camp began to recognize that we were becoming mentally stronger. Even without the ability to talk to each other openly, it was apparent to them that we were becoming a group instead of a bunch of individuals. Knowing it was harder to rule a den of young lions than a pack of whipped pups, they set out to demoralize and humiliate us. Interrogations were reinstated along with new degrading acts.

Every day at least one, sometimes two, of us would be taken to the large hooch for interrogation. In addition to the painful and brutal punishments aimed at breaking us down, we were fed large doses of propaganda. They would show us news articles of protests in the United States, calling us warmongers and baby killers. They would constantly tell us that our Government had deserted us and our fellow countrymen were staging riots against the war, denouncing us. There was no one who cared what happened to us, we were told. We were also shown each other's confessions in an attempt to turn us against one another.

Prior to this time the goons were the only ones that inflicted punishing acts toward us, but now the guards were also used in the attempt to completely degrade us. At every opportunity the guards would kick, slap, and even spit at us, and if we attempted to fend off their humiliating acts we were taken to the large hooch to learn a dose of respect.

The tactics of dehumanizing the prisoners were taking their toll. The majority of POWs began to loose interest in the escape plans. Falling into despair, they were giving up hope, saying, "There's no use." They were becoming the nothingness that they were told they were.

All this had a different effect on Alan and me, however. We began our own campaign to bring the POWs together. We kept tapping that we had to stick together and as a group, a team, we all could get through this. We insisted that no matter what the gooks did to us they could not take away our dignity unless we let them. The efforts to reunite us, however, were failing. After all, most of the

POWs had been here for a year now, and trying to convince them that someone really did care about them was difficult, to say the least.

I became rebellious towards the guards and would give them evil looks. Whenever they came around I would try to be on my feet in order to tower over them instead of allowing them to look down at me. I would stand by the door in their way, forcing them to move me, and when they would kick at me or slam their rifles into me I would show no pain and would stare at them with a 'you can't hurt me' look.

One evening when the guard was bringing my ration of rice, I stood at the door. He ordered me to step back but I just stood above him throwing daggers with my eyes. He ordered me again, and again I did not respond, so he administered a painful kick to my groin, doubling me over. He then put a spoonful of rice into my bowl, filled my water tin, and turned to leave. I was so enraged that I quickly picked up the bowl of rice and hurled it, striking him in the back of the head. He hunched forward. As he turned, his rifle butt came across my jaw, sending me against the back wall in a daze, then he called for the goons. I knew I was due for a lesson in respect.

CHAPTER 11

It wasn't but a moment before the goons were at my cage. As one jerked me from the cage the other's rifle butt caught the back of my head sending me to the floor. After a kick or two I was erected and pushed to the large hooch.

Once we reached the interrogation room I was placed in my normal position in front of the desk. The goons reported to Captain Now what I had done and took their position behind me. As always, Captain Now stood and walked to the side of his desk and with his snide sneer said, "Now lieutenant, you know I cannot allow this type of action, it would upset the entire camp. Why would you do something like this? Was there something wrong with your meal?"

At this point I knew I was in for a punishment that was to serve as an example to the others not to defy any of our captors. Even though my memory of the anguishing pain inflected on me in the past sent chills of fear through my body, my anger and increasingly intense hatred for these animals took over my actions. As I did with the guards I glared into his face, staring through his eyes, tossing daggers and said, "You fucking gook!" then spat at his face.

Instantly both goons' rifle butts impacted my body at the same time, slamming into my face and midsection. I could feel the blood spurting from my nose as I fell to the floor, gasping for air. One pulled my hand from my midsection as the other brought his rifle butt from above his head and crashed it into my fingers. The cracking of the bones sent sharp bolts of pain to my brain. They continued to pound, kick, and beat my body and head savagely for several minutes. Then as if it were a far echo I could hear the voice of Captain Now, and more guards appeared around me. They stretched me out flat on the floor, one holding my legs, one on each arm, and one holding my head down almost in a choke hold. Above me stood one of the goons with a bamboo pole about three feet long and two inches in diameter.

As he looked down at me I could tell he enjoyed his work of inflicting pain. He bent down to his knees next to me, and raising the pole above his head he then brought it down with all his might across my midsection. I tried to tense my stomach but was so weak it did no good. He swung again and again and again driving the air from my body and pulverizing my less than lean stomach muscles. The burning agony was reaching the point where it would allow me to slip into unconsciousness. Then suddenly he stopped, and everyone let go of my limbs. Captain Now approached, and stood over me. Gritting his jaws together he said, "Now lieutenant, since you did not like our rice, you will have none for three days." Then he spat down on me. The two goons drug me back to my cage and with each unable to resist the opportunity to land a few more blows, left me in a heap on the floor.

I could faintly hear Alan tapping, "How bad you hurt?" I mustered the strength to tap on the floor, "OK," and faded into the dark of unconsciousness.

The next morning as I began to stir I could hear the guards dispensing the meager portions of rice to each cage. My body once again ached beyond belief. The muscles of my stomach were so tender and weak I could barely manage to lean against the wall.

The door to my cage opened and the guard stepped in. In retaliation of being hit with my bowl, he swung a kick catching my upper leg then one to the head. He then promptly filled my water cup and wash basin, and with a satisfied smile left no rice. As he closed the door I thought, "You sons of bitches."

After the guards had left the hooch Alan asked my condition. I told him that Captain Now did not like me calling him a fucking gook and even more: "You should have seen his face when I spit in it!" I went on to tell him I was to have no rations for three days.

Alan found a way to break a couple of bamboo slats in the back lower wall separating our cages. This created a small hole about three inches by two inches that proved useful to us for the remainder of our time there. Alan passed me a portion of his allotment of rice through the hole, and for the next three days Alan shared his rice with me, cutting his own already meager ration in half.

49

My actions of throwing my bowl, and cursing and spitting at Captain Now were not acts of bravery. They were reactions of frustration and the tremendous hatred that was building inside me, and they were spontaneous, not planned. However the price paid was worth it. What was learned from my outburst proved helpful in giving motivation to the others. Alan and I began to fester the hatred for these scum bags and get everyone thinking of getting even. Never before had I realized such an intense hate and that hate was providing a real desire to survive. All our plans of escape now included malicious and evil acts against these vile and inhumane animals.

CHAPTER 12

After being in captivity now for over a year, we had gathered numerous bits of information, and one of our most detailed plans of escape was beginning to take shape. If the plan would have ever been carried out its chances of succeeding, however, would have been almost zero. Nevertheless we were busy planning every little detail. Somehow Captain Now found out that we were planning some type of escape, and one afternoon the goons appeared at my cage door.

Once again I found myself standing in front of the desk as Captain Now stood, walked to the side of it and sat on the corner. Probably because I was becoming more and more able to withstand the beatings, he began the questioning with a technique he had used with me when I first arrived. "Well now, lieutenant, how are you?"

I stood there staring at him without answering and he continued in his friendly voice, "I presume you are getting along just fine." He paused and reached down on his desk, picking up a pack of cigarettes, and held them out to me, "Would you like a cigarette?"

I hadn't had one in almost a year, since the last time he himself gave me one, but my urge was still there. I nodded my head yes and put it between my lips while he lit it. When I took the first drag of smoke into my lungs I coughed as if it were the first time I ever smoked. He looked at me with his snide smile as I took my second pull, this time doing better.

"Now lieutenant, I am disturbed about something. I have heard rumor that some of you are planning an escape. Now that bothers me because as you know escape is impossible. Besides, where would you go; your country cares nothing for you."

"I don't know of any escape plan," I responded, exhaling smoke. "Besides, you know that the prisoners here aren't allowed to talk to each other so there would be no way to make a plan."

"Now lieutenant," he said with a chuckle in his voice, "don't take me for a fool. I know of your little way of communicating. Also your name has come up in the rumor as an instigator."

I wondered if he had our code or if someone had broken, giving him the plan and me. Maybe he was just guessing, trying to get me to react; whichever it was didn't matter right now. "I don't think it would be possible to escape, so why would I plan one?"

"That's what I mean lieutenant, it would be impossible, so tell me why you are planning one."

"I'm not."

The barrage of rifle butts began, with the first one smashing the cigarette into my face. Over the next hour or so I was beaten more severely than anytime before. The crack from my ribs breaking made it almost impossible to breathe, and the blood from my face spewed everywhere. Then came the blow that kept me from perhaps being beaten to death. The rifle butt came crashing down snapping my collarbone, sending my brain more added pain than it could endure and I lost consciousness.

I began to come to life as the goons were dragging me into the hooch to redeposit me into my cage. Somehow I knew I had to warn Alan. They threw me into my cage as if I were a discarded bag of bones. I winced with pain, but immediately began to tap "QUS ESC I NO TLK G B." What I said was I was questioned about the escape plan but never told them anything, and God Bless. I heard them retrieving Alan from his cage as I again lost consciousness.

During all this time in captivity our captors were never able to break Alan. He never once signed anything nor answered any of their questions, which resulted in extremely savage beatings. He seemed to have a tremendous tolerance for pain and the ability to block it out of his mind. This tolerance and ability to block out the pain were very frustrating to Captain Now and each interrogation became more brutal. Their failed efforts to break Alan in a small way gave strength to others, but he paid a heavy price with his body.

I awoke from my unconscious state to the sound of the goons tossing Alan back into his cage. Upon their exit from the hooch I tapped to see if Alan was OK, but there was no answer. Trying to move was very painful because of my broken ribs and collarbone, but I managed to crawl to the little hole in the back of the wall. I lay on the floor, peering through the hole and attempting to visually check his condition. He was lying against the back wall in a limp pile with his face toward me. It was hard to tell if he really had a face, as it was a mass of blood and swollen completely out of shape. I tried to maneuver to see signs that he was still breathing, but the hole was too small. I prayed that he was just unconscious, and then fell back into my own state of sleep.

I drifted back to consciousness early the next morning and could barely breathe. The pain from my ribs was so sharp that when I attempted to inhale I thought that one of the ribs might be protruding into my lung. I could not use my left arm, as the pain from the broken collarbone would shoot through my body like bolts of lightning whenever I attempted to move it. With my right hand I felt my chest, checking my ribs. They felt as though they were in place but I knew that at least two were broken. I then felt my shoulder and attempted to put my collarbone in place. At times the shooting pain would almost make me pass out, but I got it in place and did my best to immobilize my arm.

After attending to the immediate needs of my wounds, I turned my attention toward Alan. When I tapped I received no response, so I eased my way to the hole in the wall. He was still in the same position, unmoved. I was beginning to worry now, because he should have at least stirred once by now. I wished I could get closer to him and check on his condition.

A noise at the front of the hooch told me that the guards were coming. I quickly rolled away from the hole as I knew that if I were caught looking through it I might be moved and if Alan was still alive he might need me when he came to. If he was still alive? The thought sent shudders through my body. Oh my God, what if that noise was them coming to get his body.

I sighed with relief when my door opened and there were the guards with my morning ration. They left my morsels of rice, filled my water can and wash basin, then left. I heard them enter Alan's cage and the footsteps walk to the back of the cage. The thud of the guard's foot slamming into Alan's body sent a chill down my spine, and then came a low moan of pain. Thank God, at least he was still alive, and I began to sob in relief.

For the next two days I was more worried about Alan's injuries than my own. He would not eat or drink and was coughing up blood. I continuously was telling him to at least drink his water but Alan would only take a few sips then set it down. This was the only time that I saw, or ever would see, Alan almost give up. Alan tapped to me once that he didn't think he would make it through the injuries this time. This caught me off guard and tears filled my eyes. I told him not to give up now, the whole camp depended on him and he couldn't let them down. I also said I needed him and he had to make it. Alan finally began to force himself to eat and gradually began to recover.

A couple of weeks later, before we went to sleep one night, I asked Alan if he was really about to give up then. He replied, "How could I? You weren't going to let me. And besides, how could I leave you alone?" I smiled to myself and fell asleep.

I became much stronger after that beating. My hate intensified and I was more determined than ever. I vowed that I would never let them break me again and they never did.

CHAPTER 13

Over the next few months things continued pretty much as they had been; there were the regular interrogations and daily doses of propaganda. They continuously would show us articles of the protests in the States, making sure to emphasize the names that the U.S. soldiers were being called. They would tell us that we were losing the war and we should quickly make our amends with them because if we didn't we would be tried as war criminals and shot. At one point, they told us that the United States Government itself had admitted that we were spies. All these efforts were an attempt to completely demoralize us, driving down any resistance that we may have, and it was working on a majority of the POWs. Most of the prisoners were concerned with just getting through each day, saying, "If no one else cares, why should we?" Soon, however, the interrogations were becoming less brutal and were containing more propaganda.

One afternoon Randy came back from an interrogation with Captain Now completely unscathed and immediately began tapping to us. He said that he wasn't asked to sign or admit to anything. Captain Now told him of the normal items of unrest in the United States, but also that we were to be transferred to Hanoi. He said that once we were in Hanoi we would either be treated very well or tried as war criminals depending on our cooperation.

Other prisoners began to be told similar stories. Alan and I began to wonder if it were true or just a ploy to get us to sign things of our own free will. Some men rationalized that the war was coming to an end and we were being taken to Hanoi to be released. Yet others believed Captain Now and began to cooperate with him. All this worried both Alan and me. We believed that no matter what the reason was, going to Hanoi would not be good for us. Also this was starting to divide the men and that wasn't good either.

Over the next few weeks Alan and I, with the help of a few others, set out to gather every piece of information that we could. When interrogated we would ask questions and sometimes get vague answers. When outside of our cages we would observe all goings on we could. From all this we concluded that the news must be true, but how would we be moved and when? We theorized that they would march us to Hanoi rather than transport us because of the influx of their troops and the lack of vehicles.

The planning at first included everyone but participation quickly declined. Everyone had different ideas as to what lay ahead in Hanoi and didn't like this or that about the plan to escape. I knew, however, that what they were saying was that they preferred life, no matter what kind, to the chance of dying. They were broken men and that angered me; it also saddened me. It came down to eleven of us who vowed that when the opportunity came we would take it no matter what. Now all we needed was a plan.

Since there were only eleven of us, the idea of overpowering the guards would not work. Elaborate ideas began to pour from our heads but none were workable. We finally trashed all elaborate schemes and thoughts of revenge, settling for a very simple, and for the most part, unplanned escape.

Not knowing where we were, there was no telling how long it would take us to march to Hanoi. We figured it was probably five days or more away, but decided we would have to make our break within three days to be safe and remain as far south as possible. We felt that the escape would have to come at one of two times. The first would be during one of their rest periods where they would stop for three to four hours to eat and rest. During this break escape would probably prove to be the riskiest as they would probably keep us bunched up and well guarded. The second opportunity would be while on the trail itself, when we were all stretched out. This period seemed to be a little less risky as we wouldn't have as far to run to cover.

The way the plan would work was when the opportunity was right or at least when Alan thought it to be right, Alan would yell, "Now!" and all eleven of us would head for the jungle at the same time. We would run into the jungle as far and fast as we could, then hide. We felt that they would not risk leaving the main body short of guards nor risk a lengthy delay in the march to search for us, and hopefully just go on. Then when it was safe we would meet up and head south together to safety.

Because of our physically unfit and weakened conditions, no one would be left to fend for himself. We would all have to work together in order to make it. Every one of us knew that not all of us would make it, in fact the odds were that none of us would. However it gave us a chance and if just one person made it, that would make it worth while. Besides, I like the other ten, preferred death to going through what we had all over again in Hanoi.

The next few nights I would lie awake and wonder about my family. Oh how I wished I knew whether my wife had a boy or girl and what it looked like. I wished that before I died I could at least see them all just one more time.

Feeling melancholy one night, I tapped to Alan and asked that if he survived and I didn't, would he look up my wife and kids. We agreed that if one made it and the other did not we would look up the other's family. However, Alan said we can't think like that. We can't think of what might happen as it might impair our actions enough to cause failure. We must only think and believe that we were going to make it.

I knew he was right. When it was time to act there would be no time for hesitation. I, however, really never thought of death itself, at that point I don't think I even feared it, but I could not keep my mind off my family. Down deep inside me, however, I knew that when it was time to break I would go.

CHAPTER 14

I awoke to the scurrying of noises around the large hooch and a constant buzzing chatter. Somehow I knew the time had come for our march to Hanoi. Knowing we would not be able to communicate much after this, I tapped to Alan and the others, "I will see you all in the jungle." Alan tapped back, telling us all to be strong, to think of and believe in our freedom and God Bless us all.

The guards were going from hooch to hooch, gathering the prisoners and assembling them in front of the large hooch. As they came through my hooch ordering us out of our cages, I stopped at my door and looked at Alan. Even though we had never been face to face before, I knew his face. We stood there for a brief moment affirming our bond with our eyes, and a warm glow filled my insides. Then the guard pushed us outside.

This was the first time that more than one of us were ever outside at the same time. As I walked where I was directed, I looked at the other prisoners. Most walked with their heads hung low, dressed in their dingy, ratty garb. Their hair hung to their shoulders and was snarled and dirty, matching their scraggly beards. Bones protruded from under their meatless skin giving them the look of a tired and beaten people. A herd of tamed animals ready to obey any command given, like robots that had no control over their being. My heart ached for them.

When we reached the large hooch we were lined up in five rows of about fifteen. I looked around, trying to get a count of the number of guards, and had to estimate the number to be about forty. Once all were in line, a hush fell over the compound and Captain Now began to speak. "Now we are all going to take a little trip and I want to explain the rules to you. First, there will be no talking at all among

58

you and that includes that silly tapping that you do. Second, you will obey every order given you immediately. If you should break either of these two rules you will be shot on the spot. Now you will be marching in a column of threes and as you can see I have more than enough guards to escort you. Also if you are unable to keep up you will be shot, and no one is to help the other." He looked around, and then barked out commands to his troops. About a dozen of his men took the lead as the rest scrambled us into columns of threes and pushed us to follow the lead guards. This was it, our trip had begun, and hopefully there would be a light at the end of the jungle.

When we were starting our second day with only two rest breaks, I could feel the heat draining what little strength I had from my body. Prisoners continuously fell to the ground only to be jerked to their feet and threatened. We were beginning to string out, spreading the guards thin.

Up ahead the trail began to narrow and there was a bend in it. Mystically, I knew that was the spot. My heart picked up speed and butterflies began to dance in my stomach. Soon now I would be free or dead.

CHAPTER 15

The break for the jungle was done by reflex, not thinking of anything but reaching freedom. Now the realization of it all was sinking in and my sobs were of mixed feelings. Fear, sorrow, and elation raced through my head as I struggled to regain my composure.

"I think they have gone on and we need to find the others. You ok now?" Alan's low whisper was broken from the lack of breath.

I nodded my head yes, knowing that our escape was not yet complete. Since we had vowed not to leave anyone to fend for themselves, we had to see if by chance the guards were wrong and others were still alive.

We both rose to our feet and made our way to the path that had been slashed by the guards. As we neared the trail, we peeked from the edge of the jungle, ensuring that no one had been left behind to look for us. After sitting there for several minutes motionless, we were sure the enemy had left and it would be safe to look for the others.

We crept along the trail, staying very close to the edge of the jungle just in case we would have to dive back into it. We found three bodies lying near the edge; they had barely left the trail before they were shot. I looked down at them, wondering which ones they were, as I knew only Alan by sight.

Just then, "Psst! Hey!" came a voice from the jungle.

I jerked my head toward the source and could make out someone emerging from the dense foliage. Then a figure appeared in the open. "Randy!" Alan said, as happy as I was to see that someone else had made it. "You alright?"

"Yeah," he replied, putting his hands to our shoulders. Then with his eyes lowered, "but Brett's back there," pointing with his head. "He didn't make it, and there's another body over there."

So far that made the count five dead and the three of us surviving. There were still three more that had to be accounted for before we could begin our journey.

"John, you look over there," Alan was pointing to the area where I had found refuge, and I quickly remembered the sounds of the guards when I was hiding. "Randy, you check over there, and I'll check over here."

I quickly scurried off in that direction. Shortly I came to where the guards had been, only feet from where I laid, and found the bloody body of their prey. Tears began to swell in my eyes again, but I knew I had no time for that now. I shook my head and wiped my eyes and continued my search. Finding nothing further, I decided to return to where I had left Alan and Randy.

As I neared the spot where I left them, Randy reemerged accompanied with another survivor, David. As we happily grasped each other's arms I asked, "How you doing?"

"Ok," he replied with a forced short smile.

Alan came back and said he found one body where he was looking, and I told them of the one I had found. Everyone now was accounted for, seven dead and the four of us. Now we needed a course of action and Alan took over, as his training as a LIRP would be needed and well made use of.

"Alright, there's only the four of us now and we need to leave all the bodies as they are and where they are," Alan began, "because if they happen to send a patrol back they may not know that anyone survived. Also, we need to leave here right away."

It was decided that we would walk along the trail, for now, in the opposite direction as before. This wasn't the safest, but in our weakened condition we didn't have the strength to go through the dense jungle and we needed out of this area. We looked around and took a moment to mourn the dead, wishing we could at least bury them properly.

"Alright, let's go." Alan said, taking the lead. "John, you bring up the rear." We filed in behind him and we were off.

The tropical heat combined with the high humidity made it seem as if we were in a steam bath. We had been walking for about an hour now and at a much faster pace than before. My mouth was parched and my legs grew rubbery. Finally we came to a place that we could get off the trail and decided to rest for a bit. We squeezed between the foliage back into the jungle and sat down.

"Anyone know where we are?" David asked.

"No," everyone replied, almost in unison.

"I figure, though, the camp was around the DMZ, or slightly north of it, and after walking almost two days that puts us well north of it," I said.

Alan was nodding his head and added, "Yeah, that's probably about right, especially since they didn't appear worried about any of our patrols around here."

"When do you think we ought to get off this trail?" Randy joined in.

"Well, it's a little risky staying on it but I don't think we could make it through the jungle. Besides, without a compass or something we would get lost and probably just go in circles," Alan answered, then continued, "Last night I noticed a fork in the trail that seemed to run off to the southeast. I think this is the Ho Chi Mien trail and that fork could be the trail they use to get down into South Vietnam. If that's the case, there should be a river just about the DMZ and maybe we can get off the trail there."

"Don't you think that they will have boats and villages on the river?" I asked.

"Yeah, but unless someone's got a better idea, we'll just have to play everything by ear."

Everyone agreed and Randy added, "Boy, that pissy-ass little bowl of rice they gave us sure would taste good right now!"

We all gave a half chuckle in agreement and Alan stated, "That it would, Randy, but I think we need to keep moving right now. We can stop around dusk and try to find something then." Alan looked at us for a moment then asked, "You all about ready?"

"Yep," I responded, "let's head for those clean beds and cold beer."

We all chuckled as we stood, then off we went.

Even in our weakened state we were able to keep up a pace about twice that of when we were going north. In our quest to find friendlys and safety, our brains were giving us an extra shot of adrenalin, making up for our lack of strength. Our search for our own had a long way to go yet, and many obstacles would be in our path, but down deep I knew nothing could stop us now.

We walked for about three or four more hours. The light began to fade to a gray, and we decided to stop. Finding a crack in the foliage we wove our way back into the jungle, maybe ten yards or so. We stopped by a cluster of jungle berries and sat down. Each of us eagerly picked the fruit, filling our mouths with the bittersweet taste that was in contrast to the bland rice we had become accustomed to. I continued to gorge myself with the harvest we had found, this time not limited by what was in my bowl.

Suddenly, "Shu!" We froze. The sound of voices came floating through the air. We fell silently to the ground and hugged it. Lying motionless and barely even breathing, we heard the voices grow closer. A group of about a dozen Vietnamese soldiers were laughing and joking with each other as they laxly walked up the trail. There was no way to tell if they were VC or NVA but we wanted nothing to do with either. Their noises began to fade as they passed, unaware of our presence.

"God Damn! That scared me!" Randy said in a half whisper after their sounds were silent.

"We're going to have to be real careful. Now that it's getting dark, there will probably be more," I stated, still afraid to breathe.

"I think we better not travel anymore tonight," Alan recommended. "We can pack ourselves in under this underbrush and hide here till morning. Besides, we need the rest."

After agreeing, we all made a nest, camouflaging ourselves with the cover of the jungle, and settled in for the night.

CHAPTER 16

All through the night we could hear troops moving up and down the trail. I knew as long as we were quiet they would have no reason to leave the trail and stumble onto us. I stayed in the same position all night for fear that they might hear the rustling of the leaves. Finally, the early morning dawn began to creep across the jungle, and the chirps and squeals of the animals filled the air. There had been no noises from the trail for an hour or so and we each rose from our nesting places.

"Am I the only one that heard them mother fuckers all night?" David asked jokingly.

"Heard who?" I asked back with a tense smile.

We all filled our stomachs with berries, then eased ourselves to the fringe of the trail. After pausing for a few minutes, we emerged and once again were in pursuit of our destiny.

Two hours later we came to the fork that Alan had seen two nights before. Taking the branch to the left, we continued at an even faster pace than the day before. The morning temperature began to rise and the muggy humidity hung like a cloud all around us. Already I was pressing my legs to keep moving; I thought to myself there would be time for resting later.

About midday we were all laboring and panting. Our desire was way ahead of our ability and strength. We decided to rest for awhile and scurried into the jungle.

As we sat trying to catch our breath, a faint noise could be heard. The sounds weren't coming from the trail, however, and didn't seem to be those of soldiers.

"Wait here and keep quiet," Alan said as he whisked off toward the noise.

When he returned he reported there was a stream and that there must be a village nearby because he had seen some children playing in the water. "I'm sure that we're still north of the DMZ so it can't be any friendlys."

Water! Boy my mouth was dry. "You think we can get upstream to where we could have some of that water?" I asked.

"Yeah. I think so." Pointing with his hand, Alan continued, "If we go over through there I think we will be safe, but I don't think we ought to stay there long."

Getting to our feet, we quietly slipped through the jungle to the stream. It was a shallow stream, but clear. We drank our fill then immersed our complete bodies in it. After semi-washing our bodies, quenching our thirst, and now feeling somewhat refreshed, we scurried back to the safety of cover in the jungle.

"Where do you think that stream goes?" Randy inquired.

"I don't know, but I think we should stay on the trail for awhile yet," answered Alan.

"Me, too," I added.

After our frolic in the water we set back out on the trail. I felt reinvigorated and had no trouble keeping pace. There still was a long way to go yet, I thought to myself, but it wasn't so far that I couldn't envision the results. I wondered if anyone would recognize me since I had lost so much weight. My mind tried to recall what the United States looked like; I bet it had really changed. Oh God, I could hardly wait to get back home!

It wasn't long before we came to a large river and it flowed toward the east, probably out into the ocean. We figured that we were now close to the DMZ but sure we were still on the north side of it. We retreated into the jungle to settle on a plan of action.

"What do you guys think?" Alan asked.

Both David and Randy shrugged their shoulders and I responded, "Well, if that is the Ben Hai River, there is going to be NVA patrol boats going up and down it, which means we can't be on the river. However, it would lead to the ocean, and just down the coast is Quangtri, and friendlys used to be there."

"Yeah," Alan interjected, "but if this is the Ho Chi Mien trail that's a long walk to the coast, being in North Vietnam."

"What if we swam across and followed it to the coast on the other side?" David inquired.

Alan responded, "It would be safer on the other side probably, but if I remember right those assholes string a lot of barb wire in the water. If we got tangled in it we would be dead."

"And the bridge on the trail is wide open. If we got halfway across it and a patrol came along we would also be dead," I added.

"What if," Randy started, "we send one person across the bridge and he goes down the trail far enough to see if anyone's coming, then the rest of us come across."

"It's still midday," I said, "and there's not a lot of charlies out on the trail this time of day. It might work."

We all agreed that was what we would do. One person would cross, then the rest would follow. Once across, we would stay close to the jungle but follow the river to the coast, then follow it to Quangtri, where hopefully there would still be friendlys. We all knew that if the one that went first was only halfway across the bridge and someone came along, he was a dead man. Now all we had to do was decide who the first person to cross was going to be.

CHAPTER 17

With each of us thinking that he should be the one to cross first, David suggested, "The only fair way to pick is to draw straws."

Using twigs instead of straws, Alan held out his hand containing the imitation straws. I drew first and chose a long one. David went second, taking another long one, and next came Randy. It was the short straw. "Does this mean I'm the lucky one?" he asked with a sheepish grin.

The bridge was about a hundred and fifty yards long. Our idea was for Randy to cross as quickly as he could and continue down the trail for about a hundred yards. There he would signal us, and if the trail was clear we would follow.

"Alright Randy, when you're ready, go for it!" Alan said, and Randy began to run. About halfway across I could see his pace slowing, but he kept right on pumping his legs. I knew that with our out of shape bodies, that distance for us was the equivalent of ten miles for a marathon runner.

Randy reached the other side and gave us the all-clear sign. We immediately set out on a dead run. Almost instantly my legs were weakening and my breath came in short gasps. We reached the other side, and all four of us lumbered into the jungle to rest, panting like dogs.

"Damn, I must be getting old," David said between gulps of air.

"You are!" I said, still winded.

After sitting there for several minutes our normal breathing began to return and Alan said, "We've got about four, maybe five, hours of light left. I think we need to get away from the trail as far as we can before nightfall. If we walk along the tree line, I think we will make the best time and still have cover."

"Do you think one of us ought to go out ahead, you know, like a scout?" I asked.

"Nah, I think we all ought to stick together. Don't you?" Alan asked.

We agreed and set out to find the coast on our mushy legs. The pace now would be a lot slower than it was on the trail.

As the shades of evening were cast upon us, we came to a place in the river where the jungle growth met the water's edge. Since darkness would soon be upon us, we decided the thick growth here would provide a safe haven for the night. Next, our attention turned to our pangs of hunger.

"I wish that I would have paid better attention in survival school," I commented.

"Me too!" agreed Randy.

"Yeah, but even in school we had a knife or something to use," David pointed out.

"There's supposed to be an abundance of food in the jungle," I added, "but like you said, without some type of gear how're you supposed to get it?"

"There should be more berries around here as close to the water as we are," Alan stated. "I guess we'll just have to make do with that for now."

"Yeah, where are them damn paradise movies when you need them?" David asked, shaking his head and making everyone laugh lightly.

We feasted on a meal of berries and quenched our thirsts with water. The sun had closed its eye and darkness was all around. In our lairs of camouflage we snuggled ourselves away for the night.

Over the next several days we followed the current of the river, winding its way through the jungle. We encountered many little villages and, believing we were still in North Vietnam, were forced to leave the bank of the river to bypass the village and rejoin the water down river.

On the start of about the tenth day, we had been walking approximately two or three hours when we began to hear gushing sounds. We stopped and listened intently.

"Unless I miss my guess," Alan began with a smile creeping to his face, "that roar we hear, boys, is the ocean!"

We looked at each other for a moment with smiles also emerging on our faces, and then broke into a fast gait. Still being cautiously aware of everything around us, we hurried toward the sound of the pounding surf.

As we broke through the foliage into the clear, Randy said, "Would you look at that!" and we all gazed at the vastness of the ocean. We stood there silently treating our eyes to the most beautiful sight imaginable. The vision of this boundless sight placed us in an awed trance.

The spell was broken with Alan's words, "Let's get back to cover guys, we're still in North Vietnam."

Still in the hypnotic grasp of the ocean we quickly ducked back to the cover of the jungle, afraid to take our eyes from the water for fear it would disappear. The sound of the surf brought us calmness, and we finally began to believe that our quest for freedom was really about to come true.

"God, that's beautiful!" exclaimed David.

"Yeah!" we all agreed.

"We still got a ways to go, though," I stated.

"Yeah," Alan agreed, "the DMZ is probably only a few miles down there. They're likely to have patrols on both sides. We're going to have to be real careful from now on."

The realization of being so close to our goal but still so far away broke the spell of the ocean. Quickly we turned our thoughts toward getting by the freedom stealing patrols.

Alan continued, "I think the best thing we can do right now is try to get south of the DMZ, don't you?"

"Yeah, if we can get past it before dark, we got a good chance of getting to Quangtri before tomorrow night," I responded.

"Well, let's get started," Randy said anxiously.

We moved rapidly but yet quietly and cautiously down the coast line, staying just inside the jungle's edge. By the time nightfall came we felt we were well south of the DMZ. We decided that we should travel inland a ways to find a safe place to spend the night. At dawn's first light we were off again.

By late afternoon we could see a village and next to it was a military compound. Elation began to build and visions of freedom filled our heads. Our joys began to diminish however as we came closer and discovered that the uniformed soldiers were Vietnamese. We believed that we were now in South Vietnam and that this compound was most likely an ARVN (South Vietnamese Army) camp, but we were somewhat reluctant to find out.

"What do you think, Alan?" I asked.

"I don't know. If they're not ARVNs, you know what will happen," he responded.

"Yeah, but if they are we can contact Americans," I added.

"Yeah, but I don't know." Alan was struggling with the decision he had made at the time of his capture, I thought.

"We got a couple of hours of light left, let's just sit here and watch for awhile," I suggested.

"Yeah," everyone agreed.

We sat there for about forty-five minutes when I heard the popping sound of a helicopter's rotor blades. "Listen," I said.

"Look!" David exclaimed, pointing to a U.S. helicopter landing at the compound.

"They are ARVNs!" Alan said excitedly.

We all jumped up and headed for the main gate of the compound. As we neared the gate, three guards demanded that we stop and held their rifles on us as the chopper took off. We tried to explain to the guards who we were and they took us to the compound commander. Again we explained who we were, and with a blank look on his face and with his Asian accent he said, "Damn."

Barking commands to one of the guards who had brought us to him, the guard quickly scampered out of the building. He returned a few minutes later reporting to the commander. The commander turned to us and said, "Gentlemen, the U.S. Army is sending a helicopter for you. They should arrive in about twenty minutes."

My feelings exploded with his words and we all began to hug each other.

"We made it!" I declared. Tears were now filling our eyes. We must have been a sight to see.

"Gentlemen, is there anything you would like while you wait?" the commander asked.

We declined, and continued with our jubilation. I still felt somewhat uneasy around Vietnamese soldiers, but also now knew I was safe. We were free! We were going home!

"Oh my God, I can't believe it!" I yelled.

CHAPTER 18

The sound of the helicopter interrupted our jubilant celebration. "Gentlemen, I believe your transportation has arrived," the Vietnamese commander announced as he began to escort us to the helipad.

As I watched the olive drab bird hover to its landing I was in ecstasy. I had been on many helicopter flights but never had I cherished a flight more than the one I was about to take. The large side door slid open and out stepped the bird's crew chief to greet us and help us aboard. Once seated, the door was slid closed and the young pilot turned, smiled and said, "We're taking you to Camp Evans, we'll be there shortly." Holding out his hand he gave us a thumbs up sign then turned and we lifted off.

Camp Evans, I thought. How fitting it was to return to the place I had left over a year and a half ago. I still couldn't believe our journey to freedom was about to end. I silently prayed, "Oh God, if this is a dream, please don't wake me up."

Darkness had settled in as we began our approach to the airfield at Camp Evans. Anxious anticipation began erupting even more inside me. As the skids touched the ground the four of us grasped our hands together and tears filled our eyes as the realization of our quest was unfolding. The squeal of the engine was winding down and the door flew open. Here was a host of people aiding us off the freedom bird and into the back of an Army ambulance. The tears were still streaming down our faces minutes later when we were greeted at the hospital with four wheelchairs.

With someone on each arm we were aided out of the ambulance and into the chairs. A colonel looked on, and once we all were seated he spoke. "I guess the appropriate thing to say is welcome home, but

72

that doesn't express what I really feel or would like to say. We are arranging for you to be evacuated first thing in the morning; these folks will take good care of you tonight. I would really like to hear your story but I won't put you through that now. However, I do need your names and service numbers."

Between sobs we gave him the requested information and he bid us a good night saying, "Boys, you have paid a great price in this war and I for one wish to say we are all in your debt. I know that doesn't ease what you must have gone through, but if there is anything that I can do for you, anything at all, just call on me."

While we were being wheeled down a corridor I thought how strange it was, we walked all that way through the jungle and now we were riding this short distance. "Damn, it feels good!" We were wheeled into a room that they were still apparently rushing around to prepare for us. It had four beds of clean white clouds and four beautiful ugly green lounging chairs by each bed. The air smelled of a cleanliness I had almost forgotten and for a moment I thought we had arrived at the pearly gates of Heaven.

Each of us had a nurse at our side taking our temperatures, blood pressures and other vital signs. They had us stand on the scale taking our weight. Sliding the weights back and forth, the nurse finally read ninety-six pounds and I sighed with disbelief. At the time of my capture I had weighed one hundred and ninety plus pounds.

"How you guys feel?" a doctor asked.

"Doc, I feel like I already died and went to Heaven!" David blurted out, causing everyone to laugh, and the sound of laughter had a great ring to it. It had been a long time since we had been around an open jovial spirit.

After asking us numerous medical questions the doctor said, "I bet you guys are pretty hungry, aren't you?"

"Are we!" we responded.

"While you're getting cleaned up I'll order some food for you. Anything special you want?"

"Doc," Alan answered, "the worst thing you have on the menu will be like a banquet to us."

"But no rice!" I quickly added.

Laughter filled the room once more. It felt so good to relax, laugh and be able to talk with all these Americans around us.

73

"Ok. No rice," the doctor said as he left the room.

One by one we were disrobed of our ratty rags and shown to the shower. "You guys don't want to keep these, eh, these clothes, do you?" one nurse asked.

"Burn them!" came the answer.

I took my turn in the shower, relishing the bliss of the moment. Lathering up, rinsing off, then lathering again, I must have washed off five more pounds of scrunge that had accumulated over the last year and a half. I stepped out and dried myself with a fluffy white towel and slipped into the soft blue hospital pajamas provided to us. The smooth cotton fabric felt so soothing to my newly clean skin. This simple everyday occurrence that people take for granted was a luxury of paradise.

As each of us finished our shower they had someone there to cut our hair and shave us. Running the clippers through our long locks, our hair was cut real short to allow them to examine for ticks and et cetera. After receiving my grooming I stood in front of a mirror looking at myself. Not being able to see my reflection for so long, I never imagined myself as I saw the others. Under my breath I cursed, "You mother fuckers!" Referring to the POW camp and my captors.

Wheeling a cart into the room a young man said, "Chow's on!" Setting us in the cushy chairs, they lowered the bedside trays to our laps. Not a word was spoken as we savored the chicken fried steak, mashed potatoes and green beans. After gorging myself with these delicacies, my stomach ached at the abundance of the serving.

"Damn, I didn't know anything could taste this good!" I said, still emptying my mouth.

"Ma'am," Randy was directing his question to the nurse, "do people really eat like this everyday?"

She giggled and responded, "Yes. Do any of you want more?"

"I couldn't eat another bite," David said.

"Me either," each of us added.

We sat, still savoring the taste of the feast, for a while then we were helped in to the fluffy beds. With all the excitement of the day's happenings, it was difficult to get to sleep. Every time a nurse came in to check on us my eyes would jet open ensuring that I was still in the hospital.

We were all awake when morning's first light crept in the window. Alan got out of bed, opened the door and walked into the hallway. Immediately a nurse was there saying, "Is there anything you need?"

"No ma'am, I just wanted to feel the freedom of opening the door and walking out it." Alan said with a satisfied smile.

The nurse gave a sympathetic smile and said, "I'd be happy to get a wheel chair and take you around if you like."

"No thanks. I just wanted to be sure I was free." He turned and came back into the room.

After breakfast we were put on a plane and flew to Camranh Bay. Here we were equally greeted and cared for. We spent two days receiving a complete physical and preliminary debriefing. We were told that we were being sent to the hospital in Japan for a couple weeks. Also our families were being notified and after our debriefing and care in Japan, they would be flown to Oakland to meet us.

Once we arrived in Japan we began our debriefing. In all phases of our care and debriefing the United States Military was extremely caring, tender, and helpful. Whenever our questioning of the events over the last year and a half was tough for us they would stop get us something to drink, rest or whatever we needed before continuing. They assured us over and over again that anything we said or signed in captivity would not be of any consequence and no one would have anything except the utmost respect for our actions. Our promotions were to take effect immediately being retroactive, and we also were to receive the bronze star. Upon our arrival in Oakland we would begin a sixty day convalescent leave. Finally, we were issued new uniforms that were tailored to our skinny frames and orders to leave for the United States. We were leaving tomorrow.

Jubilation once again erupted. We really did fulfill our quest, and found the light at the end of the jungle.

Or did we?

CHAPTER 19

As I looked out of the plane's window I could see the California coast breaking through a light haze. The 'Fasten Seat Belt' light came on as the plane began its descent into Oakland and I turned to Alan and asked, "Nervous?"

"Yeah," giving a half smile.

We knew that our families had been flown to Oakland and were to meet the plane when it landed. The whole flight I didn't doze off even once. My mind was completely on the arrival we were about to make. When we made the escape we reached for the brass ring and now we were about to claim the symbols of that ring.

My stomach had butterflies dancing and my mind rambled from thought to thought. I had dreamed every night of being reunited with my wife but now my mind wouldn't tell me what to do. How should I act? What should I say? Should I run from the plane when I see her? I searched for the answers to these questions, but my mind gave me none.

"You think there's going to be a lot of people here to greet us?" I asked Alan as the plane's wheels made contact with the runway.

"I don't know; I hope not, though. I've probably got less answers on what to do than you do," he answered, and we both gave a tense little laugh.

Randy and David were sitting in front of us and Randy turned saying, "Don't any of you go running off, I'm going to need some help." We all let out a tense releasing laugh.

"I'm more nervous now than I was when I first met my wife," David added.

"I hear that!" Alan responded.

76

The plane taxied to a stop and the other passengers began to rustle around. "Listen, no matter what everyone here has planned, none of us leaves to go back home till we have a little get together of just us and our families, ok?" Alan quickly asked.

"That sounds great to me," I said as both Randy and David nodded yes.

"Will everyone please remain seated," a voice came over the cabin speakers. "My name is Colonel Robinson, and you folks here have been privileged to have four special VIPs on this flight. I would like to allow them to disembark first. These four men are returning home after escaping from a prisoner of war camp where they were held for almost two years." A round of applause sprang through the plane and I could feel my face flush. "Will the four of you please step up here?"

"Oh God!" I said quietly. "Alan you take the lead."

"Why me?" he responded.

"Because we just voted you spokesman." I retorted.

"Bullshit! I don't know what to say."

"Don't worry we'll be right behind you," Randy added with a smirk.

"Thanks."

We stood pushing Alan out front of us, and as we walked forward another round of applause filled the plane. I felt uneasy with everyone looking at me and could tell the others did too.

When we reached the front of the plane the sharply dressed officer put down the microphone and said, "Welcome home. We couldn't arrange a large reception for you but when you get to the bottom of the ramp, off to the right you'll see some brass and your wives. It's all right to go to your wives before the brass." Smiling, he shook each of our hands and motioned us out.

As I began my exit from the plane my heart was pounding as hard as it did when I escaped. The butterflies in my stomach turned to giant bombers sending waves of excitement through my body. Walking down the ramp, I could see about two dozen soldiers in full dress uniforms standing at attention behind a major, two more colonels, and a one star general. Next to the general stood four of the most lovely women I've ever seen, our wives. They were standing with their hands clasped together under their chins and I could tell they found this as tense as we did. As we reached the bottom of the ramp the general turned to the ladies and motioned for them to go ahead to us. They all four broke into a trot with open arms.

Linda threw her arms around my neck and I tried to lift her off her feet. We kissed and hugged a long moment without a word being said. Then the colonel from the plane directed us to the group of soldiers that stood at attention.

As we began the short walk toward the general, the major bellowed, "Present arms!" and everyone's hand snapped to their foreheads. We returned the salute and the major commanded, "Order arms."

"Gentlemen," the general began, "let me be the first to welcome you home, and say how very proud we are of you. I wish there were some way to express the feeling we have for what you went through but nothing will lessen the sacrifice you have made. All I can say is that you have honored yourselves, your country, and every member of the Armed Forces of the United States of America. And now gentlemen, the colonel here will escort you to the officer's quarters where you can freshen up and have some time with your families. Tonight we have a banquet planned in your honor and tomorrow I would like to impose upon you for a little chat before you go home. Gentlemen, we salute you." His hand snapped to his brow and the major ordered, "Present arms." We returned his salute saying, "Thank you, General," and were shuffled to a small military bus with our arms around our wives.

As we boarded the bus my mind was racing a mile a minute. There were so many things to catch up on.

"Where are the kids?" I asked Linda.

"They're at home with mom, the officer that arranged for me to come here thought it best not to bring them."

"God, I can't wait to see them."

"They're excited too. They've got a party planned when you get home; we have to call and tell mom when to pick us up."

The buzzing was interrupted when the bus came to a stop. "Gentlemen," the colonel was saying, "here we are. Your wives have the keys to your rooms, and a car will pick you up tonight at twenty hundred hours. Enjoy yourselves and I will see you tonight."

With giant smiles and questions still flowing we left the bus to catch up on lost time.

CHAPTER 20

I awoke with the sun like always. I looked over at Linda lying next to me, still sleeping. Her creamy skin was so soft I wanted to reach out and touch it. I thought how good it felt to drift off to sleep with her in my arms and then awaken with her next to me. Not wanting to wake her, I decided against touching her velvet soft skin. Instead I eased out of bed, put on some clothes and slipped out of the room in search of some coffee.

Reaching the day room, I found the CQ (Charge of Quarters) brewing two pots of coffee. As I entered the room he said, "Good morning, sir, the coffee will be done in just a minute."

"Thanks," I responded. "Do you have this morning's paper?"

"Yes, sir." He left the room and quickly returned, handing me the paper, then turned to pour me a cup of the freshly brewed coffee. "Anything else that I can do for you, sir?"

"No, thanks. I'm just going to sit here a few minutes and read the paper."

The front page was completely about Vietnam. I really wanted to forget about that place for now, but couldn't resist reading the articles anyway. It talked about body counts suffered by both sides and about protests against the war effort. In not one place could I find a sympathetic or supporting statement. People who were burning their draft cards or leaving the country were being made heroes and the young soldiers risking their lives were scum. One article was about some protesters that flogged and yelled verbal slurs at returning GIs. Somehow all this didn't seem right. Didn't the people of this country know that the soldiers didn't have a choice of whether they wanted to go to war or not? That they were just doing their duty? Couldn't people realize what these young men were going through? Laying the paper down, I decided that this wasn't the norm. Tomorrow I would read of the heroic acts of soldiers.

I stood up and walked to the coffee pot. Grabbing another cup, I filled both cups and headed back to the room.

Linda was already up now, brushing her hair. "God, she looks good," I thought to myself as I said, "Honey, I brought you a cup of coffee, but I don't remember if you take anything in it."

"Thanks! I drink it just the way you do, black." She said as she stood to kiss me.

After playing our little love games, Linda and I took our showers, dressed, and set out to meet the others for breakfast. We walked across the street to the Officers' Mess where everyone was waiting on us. A special little place had been arranged for us, and we were seated together away from everyone else.

As we were being seated I said, "I'm sorry that we kept you all waiting, it's just that the shower felt so good."

Alan was thumping the table with his hand and David and Randy broke out in a quiet little laugh. David's wife, Sheila, asked what was so funny and David said, "Nothing, nothing dear," not wanting to reveal what Alan had just said with his hand.

"Barbara and I talked last night," Alan began saying, "and we thought that it would be nice if we, after our meeting with the General, all went over to San Francisco. We could get rooms there, see the sights, then have our own little celebration and go home tomorrow. What do you all think?"

"That's a great idea," I said turning to Linda. "What about it honey?"

We all agreed, and while we were meeting with the general the wives would get everything ready to leave.

At the Headquarters building a major told us that the General was expecting us and announced us. With a salute we reported to the General, and returning our salute he said, "Stand at ease men, please sit down."

We took seats and he began asking us about our future plans with the military. Telling him we hadn't decided yet, he told us of the benefits of staying in the service. After talking for about thirty minutes, he asked if we were preparing to leave today for home. We told him no and told him of our plans to go to San Francisco for the night.

"That's a great idea, but let me give you a piece of advice," the General started. "Go over to the PX (Post Exchange) and get yourselves some civilian attire first. Don't wear your uniforms in public." We asked why, and he went on to say, "You men have been gone a long time and are out of touch with the happenings here in the States. Vietnam has become a very unpopular war and people seem to vent their dislike of it against the man in uniform."

"General," I said, "I'm not ashamed of fighting in Vietnam and even the whole time I was in that cage I maintained that I believed in what we were doing. I don't understand why I have to hide that or be ashamed of it."

"Captain," it sounded strange to now be called captain, "I agree with you wholeheartedly." He paused to light a cigarette and offered us one. Alan and I accepted and he continued, "However, unfortunately there are a lot of people who don't. I've found that by not wearing the uniform in public and not talking about Vietnam you can avert an incident. Over the next few weeks you will see what I mean. I'm not saying to deny your beliefs or be ashamed of what you have done. As I stated yesterday and again last night, I personally am very proud of what you have done. Just don't confront those people out there and get yourself in trouble."

We left the General's office and I still didn't quite understand his advice. To some degree in all wars not everyone is always behind the involvement of their countries, but the issue of whether we should or should not be in Vietnam can't be blamed on the individual soldier. Can it? Doesn't every soldier have the responsibility to support and comply with the decisions of his country?

"What do you guys think of his advice?" I asked as we left the building.

"Hell if I know," Alan said, shaking his head.

"I guess we ought to get some civvies though, like he said," replied David.

On the way back to the Officers Quarters, where our wives were, we stopped at the PX and purchased some clothes to wear to San Francisco. When I returned to the room, Linda was almost finished packing our things and stopped to give me a hug and a kiss.

"What's in the bag?" she inquired.

"Oh, some civilian clothes. The General advised against wearing uniforms in public," I answered.

"That's a good idea, I was going to suggest that, but didn't know how to tell you."

"Why shouldn't I wear my uniform?"

"Well, people aren't happy with the way the military is slaughtering those people."

"What do you mean?"

"Oh, honey, let's not talk about it right now," she said as she turned away to finish packing.

My gut wrenched as if a blow had struck me there. How can she of all people say words like that? Why did everyone think we were the ones that were wrong? And what does everyone mean, 'the way we were slaughtering those people'? Didn't people know about the things those gooks did to us? The gooks were the ones that were inhumane, not us. How could the public be so uncaring? Nothing made any sense to me, and little did I know that it never would make sense again.

CHAPTER 21

After our San Francisco excursion we each boarded a plane for our homes. Making sure we each had addresses and phone numbers we agreed to talk to each other in a couple weeks. While on the plane I couldn't help but feel some remorse. I had been with these fellow escapees everyday for over a year. Now suddenly a lonesome feeling was overtaking my being and even with all the people on the plane and my wife next to me, I felt isolated. I told myself when I got home things would be different and the feeling of isolation would go away.

The plane landed and taxied to the gate. As Linda and I departed the plane I could see my mother in law holding my youngest son, Matt, and holding the hand of my oldest son, Richard. I ran to where they were taking Matt in my arms and squatting down to hug Richard. I was amazed at how big they were. When I left Richard was almost two years old and of course Matt was born about the time of my capture.

"Daddy why didn't you come home sooner?" Richard asked.

It took everything I had to hold back the tears that were welling in my eyes when I answered, "I wanted to son, but I'm here now. And we're going to have lots of fun together, aren't we?"

As we drove home I held both my boys and tried to answer their many questions. When we reached our destination Linda's family was there and the house was decorated with balloons and signs that the boys had colored. "That one says welcome home daddy." Richard told me.

"And it's beautiful." I said unable to hold back my joy.

"Why are you crying daddy?" Asked Richard.

"I'm just so glad to be home son."

For the first time in two years I tucked my children in bed at night. Hugging them before turning out their light sent emotion through my body that could never be put into words.

Over the next couple weeks I filled the days with entertaining the boys. We went to the park, zoo, lake and every where they wanted to go. With the days consumed with getting to know my sons the evenings were filled with everything Linda had organized. Every night she either had friends over or we met them out. It seemed that every minute was planned out and occupied with some type of activity. I felt like a hollow shell of a person just doing what was expected without really being there. I yearned to just be alone without anyone around.

One afternoon when the boys and I returned from a day at the park Richard asked Linda, "Mama why doesn't Uncle Bill come over any more?"

Linda's face took on a look of shock and quickly shuffled Richard off to clean up for dinner.

"Who's Uncle Bill?" I asked after Richard left the room.

"Just a friend." She replied turning and walking away.

I followed her as she headed for our bedroom. "Why did Richard call him uncle?"

Tears began to fill her eyes as she explained that she had gone to high school with him and after I was reported missing in action she ran into him while out with some friends. She continued to say that he started coming by a lot and would take her and the boys on outings together. "He wanted me to marry him but the moment I found out you were alive and coming home I broke up with him."

Marry him? I tried to imagine how tough it must have been on her when she was notified I was missing, and not knowing if I would ever come back. Yeah it probably was tough on her but it was tough on me too. She was still talking but I couldn't hear as my mind began to flash images of Captain Now and the goons. I winced thinking of the pain and began to feel very hot. Shaking my head to try and lose the images in my head, I turned and walked outside to sit in one of the chairs on the patio. I began to tremble and beads of sweat popped out all over my forehead.

"John." "John." I could barely distinguish her words as I turned my head to look at her standing there. "John, are you all right?"

"Yeah." I said as the images began to fade.

"John, I'm sorry. I promise I'll never see him again, ok?"

"Ok." I responded. "I think I'm going to take a shower now." I said as I stood up. I felt weak and dizzy.

"Are you sure you're ok?" She again asked.

"Yeah."

That night I couldn't sleep. I got out of bed without waking Linda and again went to sit on the patio. The cool night breeze caressed my body as I tried to think through my emotions. I had so many different feelings inside me, and they were at war with each other. I felt happy but yet sad, crowded but yet alone, safe but yet afraid, compassion but yet anger. I wanted to laugh but felt more like crying. I wanted to talk but couldn't.

The sound of the birds tweeting reveille for the sun brought me out of my deep thoughts. Looking at the big ball of fire climbing above the horizon, I knew that I had sat there all night. I went into the kitchen, made some coffee and returned to the patio to watch the birds soar high above in the red streaked blue sky.

Later that day Linda was going to go over to her mothers and asked if I wanted to join them. I told her no I just wanted to sit around and relax and asked if she would mind taking the boys with her.

"Are you still upset with me?" She asked.

"No I'm not upset with you."

"You didn't sleep at all last night. What's wrong?"

"Nothing's wrong. I just wasn't tired. Now run along and have a good visit, ok?"

Gathering the boys she kissed me and was on her way.

I was still sitting on the patio when I realized the phone was ringing. Reluctantly I went inside and answered it.

"Hello."

"Hey buddy, how you doing?"

A smile came to my face. "Hey Alan. I'm great. How about you?"

"I'm probably about as great as you."

"Yeah, probably so. What are you up to anyway?"

85

"Listen John, I need to get away for awhile so I thought I might take off and go fishing for a few days. Thought you might want to come along. You know just the two of us. What do you say?"

"Sure! But where we going to go?"

Alan went on to say he knew a place to go stream fishing in Colorado. We agreed to meet on Friday and hung up.

A kind of warmness filled my insides as I called the airlines to make my reservations. This just might be what I need, I thought. Now if Linda would only understand and not be upset that I would be gone for a few days.

CHAPTER 22

It was late evening when I arrived in Colorado. I grabbed a cab and went to the hotel where Alan said we would be staying. When I checked in, I asked the clerk if Alan had checked in yet. "Yes sir, he's in room two eighteen, just down the hall from you," he said, handing me a key. I went to my room and deposited my suitcase and fishing gear, then went down the hall to room two eighteen.

Alan answered my knock with a big smile and we embraced each other. It seemed like a year instead of a month since we had seen each other. I immediately began to feel safe and not quite so alone.

"Hey, there's a great little lounge just down the street and I've already rented us a car. What do you say we go get us a drink, huh?" Alan was already headed for the door when he asked.

We found a corner table, sat down and ordered a couple scotch and waters. "God damn! I'm glad you came. I thought I was going to go crazy. I wanted to talk but couldn't; besides, no one wanted to listen anyway. You know what I mean?" Alan asked, fidgeting with the straw in his glass.

"I damn sure know what you mean," I answered, thinking of all the confusion I had inside me.

We continued to order drinks as we each took turns listening to the other. Right then it seemed easy to tell each other how we were feeling. Whether it was the scotch or the fact that we understood the other's emotions where nobody else could, I don't know, but it sure felt good. We stayed till the place closed then returned to our rooms a little less tense.

The next morning we were at the stream's edge at first light. The cool mountain air soothed my achy head. As we gathered our tackle from the car, Alan said, "You know if it weren't for these pine trees this would almost look like that stream back there."

I looked around and knew he was talking about the stream we had encountered on our escape. An eerie feeling crept through my bones as I answered, "Yep."

"Hell, let's catch breakfast," Alan said, and we both laughed as we walked to the fishing hole.

During the next few days we drank a lot of beer and only managed to catch a few fish. By Monday afternoon we knew that it was time to return home. I hated to leave the peacefulness, but I also knew my leave would soon be over and I still needed time with my family. Alan and I said our goodbyes and once again went our different directions.

Linda was at the airport to pick me up when I arrived home. She greeted me with a giant hug and kiss and asked, "Where's the big catch you were going to get?"

"I had one this big," holding my arms far apart, "but they wouldn't let me bring it on the plane. They said it weighed too much."

"Sure you did," she responded, with both of us laughing as we headed for the car.

"Where are the boys?" I asked, and she replied that her mom had them. Her mom had taken them to some function for children at the library and would bring them home later.

When we arrived home she handed me a large manila envelope. "This came the other day for you."

It was from the Department of Defense and I quickly opened it, knowing that it was my orders. "I've been assigned to Fort Rucker, and I'm supposed to report there on the twenty-ninth. That's about three weeks from now."

"You know, we haven't talked about what you're going to do, John. Are you going to stay in the service and, if so, what about us?"

"What do you mean, what about us? If I stay in you go with me, right?"

"I kind of hate leaving here, but I think that we need to be together if we want us to work. Do you want to stay in?"

"I don't know. It's probably the best thing to do right now, though."

"Well, if we only have three weeks, we'd better start packing and arrange for the movers, right?"

"Let's start later when the boys get home. Right now do you realize we are all alone?" I asked as she fell into my arms.

The next couple of weeks seemed to go by quickly. We were busy every day packing everything up and preparing to leave. Her mother would look after the house for us, as we had decided to rent it out rather than sell it. We also decided we would leave a few days early so I could help her find a place for us to live.

"The movers will be here tomorrow, you know," Linda announced to me one afternoon.

"Yeah. I think we have everything ready, don't you?"

"Yes, but would you mind if I meet my friends for awhile tonight? I'd like to say goodbye to them, and they wanted to take me out for a little while, ok?"

"Where're you going?"

"Oh, I don't know. I won't be late, though. Do you mind?"

"No, I don't mind. Go ahead and have fun," I said with a smile.

Later that evening I put the boys to bed, then opened a beer and sat on the patio. I wondered how it was going to feel to be back in the sky again. I really did miss flying. What if, I thought, they don't let me fly anymore? After all, it's had been almost two years since I'd been behind the controls of an aircraft. Certainly they would allow me to fly, I told myself. And if they didn't, the hell with them! I'd get out. But then what?

Still wrestling with these questions, I went to the refrigerator for my sixth or seventh beer. The clock said two-ten am. Where's Linda, I wondered. She said she wouldn't be late; I wonder if something has happened to her. I decided not to call around. Besides, I didn't know where to call anyway. I returned to the patio, saying to myself: she'll be home anytime now.

CHAPTER 23

When we arrived at Fort Rucker we checked into a hotel and began looking for a house. The second day of our search we found one that Linda really liked and made the arrangements to rent it. We called the movers to see if our household goods had arrived yet and they had. The movers agreed to deliver everything the next day, the twenty-ninth, the day I had to report in.

The next morning we checked out of the hotel and I drove Linda and the boys to the house we had rented. She was going to wait there for our things to be delivered. "They probably won't have me doing much today, so as soon as I get checked in and squared away I'll come back and help you with everything. Ok?" I asked.

"Ok," she answered, giving me a hug and a kiss to send me on my way. "Good luck."

"Yeah."

When I arrived at the main gate the guard stopped me, asking me my business on the post. I told him I was to be assigned here, showing him my orders, and he gave me a temporary pass. "How do I get to HQ to report in?" I asked, and he gave me directions.

Upon reaching battalion headquarters, I was directed to see Major Edwards. "Good morning, Major. I was told that I needed to report in to you," I said, handing him a copy of my orders.

"Captain Walker, ah yes. How are you?"

"Fine, sir."

"We have been expecting you, Captain," the major was saying as he pointed to a chair by his desk. "Sit down."

"Thank you, sir."

"You know, the Colonel and I were discussing you last week when we received word that you were arriving. You have your two-o-one file?"

"Yes, sir," I responded and handed him the folder.

"You've been through some real hell, haven't you?"

I responded with only a small smile and a single nod of my head.

"The old man is eager to meet you, but first we need to decide what we're going to do with you."

"I don't understand, sir. What do you mean, what you're going to do with me?"

The major chuckled and continued, "Nothing bad, Captain. It's just that you haven't flown in a long time and aren't current. Also you don't have any command time, not that you have had the opportunity. But we need to decide what your intentions and desires are, and then find something that will best suit you and us. Do you know what you would like to do, Captain?"

"Well, sir, I'd like to get back to flying, and as far as career goals I'm not sure what I have to do."

"There's a class starting next week that would get you current if that's what you want."

"I'd like that, sir."

"Great. I'll get you in that class then the old man and I can decide what position to put you in. I'm sure you're going to be a great asset to us. Welcome aboard, Captain," the major said, holding out his hand to shake mine. "Now let's see if we can get you into see the old man, come on."

I followed the major down the hall to the outer office of the Battalion Commander. "Sparky, is the old man busy?" the major asked the clerk behind the desk.

"He doesn't have anyone in there right now, sir," the clerk answered.

"Fine. Captain, have a seat and I'll see if he can see you now," the major directed as he entered the colonel's office.

Shortly the major returned, telling me to come in. I staunchly walked in. Coming to attention in front of the colonel's desk and saluting I said, "Sir, Captain Walker reporting."

The colonel returned my salute and told me to stand at ease. "Well, Captain, Major Edwards tells me that he is impressed with you already."

"Thank you, sir."

Looking at my file in front of him that must have just come from the major, he said, "I see here, Captain, that you have received a number of medals and I'm sure that you have earned every one of them. But tell me, Captain, why aren't you wearing them on your uniform?"

His question caught me off guard because I had a lot of mixed feelings about them. I didn't feel like telling him all the reasons right then, so I told him that I just hadn't had the time to fix up my ribbon bars yet. He accepted that, then asked if I had brought my family with me. I told him I had, and he said he would have his wife get in touch with mine to help her get settled in.

After about fifteen minutes of questions and answers, the colonel told me that it was good to have me there and he looked forward to good things. I thanked him, saluted, and left his office. Walking back down the hall, the major told me to take the rest of the day to get my personal things done and to report to him in the morning. "And also Captain, as you saw, the old man is big on wearing medals earned. I suggest that you take care of that right away," he said, once more shaking my hand.

I left the post, heading for our new home to help Linda. My mind was on the statements made about my medals. In some ways I was proud of my actions to earn them, but in other ways they could never make up for what I had gone through. More than the issue of the medals themselves, however, I was becoming confused. On one hand you were expected to wear all these symbols of the war, but on the other hand you must keep it quiet in public. How could you be proud of something if you have to hide it?

After the two week pilot refresher course I was certified as up to date and current. Flying meant so much to me as it was an escape. It gave me the sensation of leaving all my cares on the ground when I lifted off.

I was assigned to Bravo Company as the operation officer. Major Edwards had told me of his high hopes for me and said that he would get me into a command position as soon as he could. I wasn't interested in a command position, however; in fact I really didn't want one. All I wanted was to do my job, be left alone and fly as much as possible.

I envied the warrant officers as their primary responsibility was, for the most part, just to fly. Soon I began to hang out with the WOs and shun any association with the brass. More and more, after duty hours, I could be found at the Blade and Wing, the Officers' Club bar, drinking with the WOs. These actions along with my lack of initiative in seeking additional tasks and responsibilities, doing only what was required, were causing me to loose popularity at Battalion. Their hopes of me being one of their crack officers began to fade and Major Edwards started riding me about this and that.

Every day the paper was full of protests against the war and every article was putting down the efforts of the war and the soldiers themselves. I associated with no civilians and began to spend all my time on post, never venturing into the civilian public. Still I found myself a mass of confusion as to the military's attitude of hiding their existence off-post and flaunting it on-post. I began to harbor ill feelings against civilians for denouncing the soldiers and against the military for wanting me, while on post, to flaunt my symbols of war, and began to rebel against both.

Seven months went by before my first big trouble-causing incident took place. As I was leaving the Officers' Club one evening I was still dressed in my flight suit, and once outside I still hadn't put on my hat. A non-aviator major stopped me and told me to put my hat on. He asked if I was in the habit of not saluting. As I stood there looking at him, there was something that I just didn't like about him. Maybe it was the feelings I had at that moment toward the military or maybe it had something to do with me having too much to drink. At any rate I wasn't in the mood to play games and said, "Fuck you, major," and began to walk away. He grabbed my arm and asked in a rude commanding tone, "What's your unit, Captain?" Grabbing my arm was a mistake because I turned and landed my fist in his face.

The next morning I was called to battalion and the colonel wasn't happy at all. "Captain, I realize you have gone through some tough times. However, that does not excuse your actions of late. Now maybe you are having some trouble readjusting and I'm willing to forgo a court martial for your latest incident here on one condition.

That condition is that you report to the hospital and seek some counseling. I also want you to understand that I will not tolerate any more of this behavior no matter what your past, do you understand me?"

"Yes sir," I replied, still standing at attention.

"I'm going to call the hospital right now and I expect you to report there this afternoon. Understand?"

"Yes, sir."

"That's all, Captain. I expect to see improvement here. Dismissed."

I reported to the hospital and was set up with one of the psychiatric counselors for daily counseling. Every day this guy would sit there with my records in front of him, asking me questions to which I would answer yes, no, or I don't know. How could he expect me to tell him how I felt inside? I knew he could not understand nor did he really care. No one could understand nor did any one care. No one, that is, except Alan. We had talked a couple of times on the phone and he was having trouble coping, too. We agreed that no one could understand what we felt and it looked like no one cared. Sometimes we didn't understand how we felt or why we felt that way.

From the time I hit that major things went downhill. I became the problem child of the battalion, receiving many reprimands ranging from disrespect to disobeying orders to being kicked out of counseling for striking the counselor. By the way, the order that I disobeyed was not wearing my medals on my dress uniform.

During this time my antics were causing a lot of stress between Linda and me. It seemed the more we argued the more trouble I got into and the more trouble I got into the more we argued.

One afternoon I was told that Major Edwards wanted to see me ASAP. My first thought was, "Damn, now what did I do?" I was beginning to think that this was not for me and I should do something else, but didn't know what.

The major began, "Captain, you have been in this unit now for a year. It's time for your efficiency report and I can't find one good thing to put in it. What's your problem, Captain?"

"I don't have a problem, sir."

"Oh yes you do. What do you purpose I put in this report?"

"I don't know, sir," I responded. Then suddenly a thought came to mind and I spoke. "Sir, I wish to request a transfer."

"What good will that do you, Captain?"

"Well, sir, that probably would be best for both the unit and myself, sir."

"With that I agree, Captain. Have your request on my desk in the morning. That's all, dismissed."

CHAPTER 24

I picked up the forms that I needed from the company clerk and headed home early. Now that I had opened my mouth I didn't have much time to decide where to be transferred to. One of the WOs had told me about a couple of overseas assignments that sounded like good duty, but I didn't know how Linda would react to going overseas. For that matter, I didn't know how she was going to react to any transfer.

When I arrived home, Linda was watching her soap opera on TV but quickly turned it off when I walked in. "What's wrong?" she asked.

"Nothing's wrong. Why do you think something's wrong?"

"Because you're never home at this time of day. Now, did something happen?"

"Well, yes something happened but it's not all that bad," I said. Then setting my paperwork down on the kitchen table and opening a beer, I told her of the meeting with Major Edwards and the request for transfer.

I was kind of surprised when she responded, "That might be best. But where will we go?"

"I don't know yet. I was thinking that it might be best to go overseas for a while. What do you think of that? I think I'd like to get away from everything that's happening here in the States."

"Are you saying you want to get away from me, too?"

"No, no. See, one of the guys told me of an assignment in Thailand. Now it's only a one year tour."

Interrupting me she asked, "That means it's a hardship tour and you go without dependents, doesn't it?"

"Yes and no. Let me finish will you?"

"Ok, ok. Finish."

"As I said, it's only a one year tour, but what I was told is that there are a lot of families there. The assignments in Bangkok are two year accompanied tours. Now what I thought was that I would request to go to the unit just north of Bangkok for the one year tour, then pay your way over. The military won't pay your way, but we can afford that. What about it?"

"Is it a safe place? You know the boys are pretty young."

"I'm sure it's safe. Plus, this way we will only be gone a year and back to the States so Richard can start school in this country."

We discussed the idea for over a hour and finally decided to try it. If it wasn't a good place for her and the boys, they could always come back before me. I quickly called the post and found out what unit was there and the other information I needed to complete my request.

The next morning I went to Major Edwards with my request. As he looked it over he said, "You know, Captain, that is a Special Forces unit and it's a hardship tour."

"Yes, sir, I do. But I understand that they have an aviation company and are in need of company grade officers."

"All right, Captain. I've got a friend at DA, I'll call him today and see what can be done. You know, of course, I still can only give you a mediocre efficiency report."

"Yes sir, I understand."

The next day Major Edwards called and told me he had spoken to his friend in DA. The assignment was mine if I was willing to be there in forty-five days. That wouldn't give me much time for a leave and travel but if I wanted I could have it. I told him I would take it and he said he would have my orders cut tomorrow. He also said that I would need all the time I could get to prepare, so as of that moment I was officially relieved of my duties. I thanked him, quickly gathered my things and set out for home to tell Linda.

I once again surprised Linda by being home so early in the day. She listened to what I had to say, and then gasped, "That's not a lot of time."

"That's right, and we have to make a lot of plans quick."

The limited time we had would not allow for Linda to get her passport and visa before time for me to report in. This meant my family would not be able to travel with me. We decided that we could store all our household goods at her mother's and she could stay there till she received her passport and visa. I would go on ahead and get a place for us to live. Then when she received her travel papers she would fly to Bangkok where I would pick her up. Linda was beginning to like our plans and eagerly helped to set them in motion.

Within a week arrangements to ship our household items to her mother's were made and passport applications for her and the boys were submitted. When the movers picked up our things I checked out of my unit and our new adventure began.

CHAPTER 25

I arrived in Thailand two days prior to my report-in date, and decided to report in early. I found my way to HQ and was directed to the captain in charge of personnel. He greeted me, telling me his name was Mike and that they had only received word of my assignment there two days ago. Immediately I sensed a friendlier air here than in the unit I had just left.

"Come on John, let's get you in to see the old man," Mike said, already walking out his office.

As I entered the commander's office, he arose from his desk. He was tall and muscular with a touch of gray creeping into his hair. His smile said he was an easygoing and cordial person, but it was easy to see he could be stern and tough if necessary. I reported to him and he returned my salute in a lax manner, then held out his hand to shake mine and told me to have a seat. I sat quietly for a moment while he looked through my file.

"You got a hell of a file here, Captain. Let me first say, it's John isn't it?" I nodded yes and he continued, "let me first say, John, we only have a small aviation detachment here. You'll be assistant to Will Dixon, he's in charge of the detachment. We are authorized two captains and four warrant officers and have four aircraft. Right now you will fill the second captain's slot and we're still short one warrant slot. That means you will have to do a lot of the flying yourself."

"That's no problem, sir," I interjected.

"Ok. This unit has a tough job, John. It takes everyone working together to get it done, and security here is a major concern. I expect my officers to complete their jobs without someone looking over their shoulders all the time. I allow my men to play hard but I expect them to work equally hard. Now, I'm not holding any of these reprimands

99

here against you, just as you won't get special treatment for what you've been through. All I ask is you do your job, and let me say this: instead of a reprimand if you haul off and hit one of the officers here, you'll probably get one hell of a fight," he chuckled.

"Yes sir. I'll do my job," I said.

"One question, John."

"Yes, sir."

"Why, after being away from your family for so long, did you request a hardship tour?"

I explained my plans for Linda to join me, and he said, "That's fine, several of my officers have their families here. One thing however, since this is a hardship tour, no special consideration will be given just because you have your family nearby."

"I understand, sir."

"Now, Mike has his wife over here; I'm sure he would be glad to help you get settled in. You need to go see the airfield and get acquainted with things, Mike will see to that. I've got an officer's call tomorrow at seventeen hundred hours. You will meet everyone then."

As I left his office my salute was once again returned in the same lax manner as the first one. Once outside his office, Mike said, "Let's get a jeep from the motor pool and I'll show you around."

While showing me around, Mike offered his services to help me get settled in. He said my wife would have no problem as there were eight others and they really helped each other. He also offered to let me stay at his house, which I accepted, and said he would help me find a place for my family.

The next evening the officer's call was held at the Officers' Club. Mike introduced me to most of the officers as we had a drink and waited for Colonel Myers to arrive. "Will, this is your new assistant, John Walker," Mike said introducing me to the captain in charge of the aviation detachment.

"Hi, how you getting along?" he asked.

"Fine. I'm ready to start," I said.

"Good. If you survive this tonight, I'll expect you at the airfield in the morning. I can sure use some help," he said with a big smile.

"What do you mean if I survive tonight?"

"You'll find out."

The Colonel arrived and walked to the front of where we stood. "All right, gentlemen, let's get started." He went on making different announcements and after about ten minutes said, "Now we have a new member to welcome." Motioning for me to come to the front, he continued, "This is Captain John Walker. He's going to be helping Will out at the airfield. As tradition has it, John, we will buy you your first official drink here."

I half smiled as the waitress appeared with a large water glass full of a red substance, which I later learned was half tequila and half Tabasco sauce, and a large Morton's Salt box. A major stepped forward and took the items as the Colonel said, "You need to watch out now; according to Captain Walker's records he has a habit of hitting majors." Every one laughed as the major said, "Oh, yeah."

The major instructed me to take off my watch and lick my arm from my elbow to my wrist getting it as wet as possible with saliva. After I complied he took the Morton's Salt container and poured salt on my arm until it would hold no more. "Now Captain, you are to eat all the salt and I mean all, then chug this drink then suck on a lemon. After you're finished you can address every one. You ready?"

I nodded and he said, "Go!"

I ate all the salt and my mouth began to pucker, then put the glass to my lips. As the fire went down my throat all the other officers were counting in unison, "One thousand one, one thousand two, one thousand three." When I finished the drink my mouth and throat were on fire, and I quickly put the lemon in my mouth, thinking it would reduce the heat of the fire. A second burst of flames flashed through my mouth. The lemon had been soaked in hot sauce!

The major stepped forward again and said, "Captain, you are now a member of the Special Forces and you may speak to us all now."

I had no breath, my mouth was ablaze and sweat was pouring from my forehead, but managed a course, "Hi."

Everyone laughed and cheered as first the major said, "I'm Jack, welcome," as he shook my hand then each officer filed by, shaking my hand and introducing himself.

The next morning Will was knocking at the door of the two story, three bedroom bungalow I had rented the day before. "Hey, John, you still alive?" He asked, laughing.

"Yeah, but God damn my head hurts."

He laughed again and said, "They're a rowdy bunch, but a lot of fun. Come on, I got the jeep outside to take us to the airfield."

When we arrived at the airfield he showed me the birds and their records, then where my office would be. He told me that I would be in charge of scheduling the missions and who would fly them. He also said that only one of us would be gone at a time unless absolutely necessary. After we had gone through everything he said, "Now let's take an orientation flight," and off we went into the sky.

About a week later I received my first letter from Linda. It said she had received her passport and was trying to make flight arrangements. I decided that it would be best to talk to her by phone rather than by letter so I went downtown to the prehistoric phone company. I told them I wanted to place an overseas collect phone call and gave them the number. About an hour later the lady there directed me to a small both where my call was put through.

The connection wasn't very good but it was still good to hear Linda's voice. I told her I had found us a house and described it. Linda said all the arrangements to leave were made. They were to get their vaccinations the next day and would leave in three days. She gave me all the flight numbers and pertinent information of her arrival and I told her I would meet them. We then said our goodbyes and hung up.

I went directly from there to the Officers' Club where I knew Will would be. I ordered myself a drink and told Will of Linda's arrival in Bangkok on Friday. "You think there would be any problem with me taking the day off?" I asked.

"There shouldn't be any problem, John. In fact I don't think there's anything going on this weekend, why don't you take the weekend off and spend the night in Bangkok. I'll cover everything here."

"Thanks!" I said, raising my glass to him.

CHAPTER 26

My family arrived at Dong Mong airport Friday afternoon and I was there to meet them. After they were checked through customs we went to the Chopia Hotel in downtown Bangkok. The Chopia Hotel was used by the military as Officer Quarters for officers in transit or in Bangkok for short periods. Linda was amazed at how nice it was, and also how modern Bangkok seemed. "I was expecting some backwoods country with outdoor plumbing," she said.

"Bangkok is very modern, honey, but we live about a hundred miles north of here and it's not quite like Bangkok."

"You mean we have outdoor bathrooms there?"

"No, no, it's not that bad, but it's not Bangkok. You'll like it, though. I promise." I told her about the house and the town, and when I said she would have two house girls she really thought it would be all right.

We spent Friday night at the hotel, then took the boys out Saturday to see the sights. That afternoon, tired from sight seeing, we took the train north to our new home. Linda liked the house I rented, and settled right in. The other wives came by on Sunday and before long she was part of their little club. It also wasn't long before she was spoiled by having two house girls to do everything for her.

I was flying every second or third day and working at the airfield the rest of the time, but there was plenty of time for Linda, the boys, and myself to do things as a family. There wasn't any TV so two or three times a week we would go to a movie. We got together with the other American couples for outings or to play cards. I was beginning to loose the hostile feelings that I had been harboring. For the most part I was a normal person and feeling like one. I was getting along with every one and not getting into trouble. These were probably the best months Linda and I had since my return from Vietnam.

Then suddenly the roof caved in. I received word that HQ wanted me ASAP. When I arrived, Mike said the old man wanted to see me and that he had an emergency communiqué for me. "What about?" I asked.

"I don't know, but go on in," Mike answered.

I knocked on the Colonel's door and was told to come in. He returned my salute in the same lax manner as always and told me to set down. "John," he began, "I've been in the military for over twenty years, in peace and war. I know the bonds of war sometimes mean a lot to a man and that's why I wanted to tell you of this myself."

"I don't understand sir. Tell me what?"

"I received an emergency communiqué today from a Captain Alan Wilson." My heart leapt to my throat and my stomach twisted as I knew something was wrong. "One of the men you escaped with, David Hanson, is dead. I'm sorry."

My entire body felt numb, and tears began to well in my eyes. "How? What happened?" I tried to ask.

"I don't know. But if you need leave, you've got it and if there is anything else I can do just let me know."

"Yes sir, I'll have to go. Is there some way to send Alan a message?"

"No problem. I'll have Mike take you home to get some things together and then I'll have Will fly you to Bangkok to catch a flight. If you want to leave your family here I personally will make sure they're looked after."

"I don't know, sir. I'll have to talk to my wife first," I said as I tried to get to my feet. My legs were trembling so bad that I almost collapsed. The Colonel took hold of my arm and called for Mike to take me home.

When I arrived home Linda could see that something was not right. She asked what was wrong and I told her saying, "I have to go there."

"I understand."

I asked if she wanted to go also or stay here. I told her that the Colonel said he would make sure she was looked after if she stayed.

Linda asked how long I would be gone and I said, "I don't know. A few days, maybe a week." She decided it would be best to stay there and wait for me.

Linda quickly helped me pack then Mike drove me to the airfield. Will was already there and ready to fly me to Bangkok.

When I landed in Columbus, Alan met me at the airport. "Alan," I said as we embraced. "What the hell happened?"

"He killed himself, John."

"Bullshit!" I was in shock. "Why?"

"He's had it real tough lately. He hasn't been able to get a job in almost a year now, and his wife left him a little over a month ago."

"Why didn't he tell us?" I said as we got into the car that Alan had rented.

"I don't know. He left a note and said to tell you, me, and Randy he was sorry but he just couldn't take any more."

"God damn. Is Randy here?"

"Yeah, he's back at the hotel. He's not taking this well, either."

"When's the funeral?"

"Tomorrow."

When we arrived at the hotel we went straight to the room. Randy was just sitting there sobbing, and stood when we entered. "John." He said giving me a hug. "I don't understand."

"I don't either, Randy, I don't either."

Alan walked to a cooler he had and took out a couple of beers, "You want one?"

"Yeah," I responded.

"I talked to him a couple of weeks ago and he was real upset about Sheila, but I didn't think it was this bad," Randy sobbed. "If I would have known I would have been here."

"We know, we all would have," Alan responded.

The three of us sat up all night, drinking and talking. I could feel the rage and hate beginning to build up again inside me. I couldn't understand why. We had been through so much, why?

The next morning we took our showers and began to dress. Alan and I decided that we would wear our dress uniforms and Randy was wearing a suit since he wasn't in the service anymore.

"I don't know if it's such a good idea to wear these uniforms, John," Alan said.

105

"Why?"

"Those people out there."

Anger swelled inside me, "Fuck those pussy ass wimps!" I said. "I haven't done anything I'm ashamed of and if they want a piece of my ass, bring it on."

"Yeah. They sure as hell haven't done anything for us, have they?"

After the funeral, as we were driving back to the hotel I said, "I need a Goddamn drink. Let's stop somewhere and get one."

We found a little lounge that looked quiet and went in. We each ordered, and the bartender looked at Alan and me like we were freaks. I glared at him and he served us. Halfway through our drinks I could hear a group of guys a couple of tables away from us talking to each other about the big bad GIs. Red flashed through my head and I stood, throwing my glass right at them, "That's right mother fucker, big and bad. You want some of it assholes? Come on."

They got shocked looks on their faces, but just sat there. Alan and Randy stood at my side and all three of us stood there staring right at them. The bartender came over and told us to leave. Alan looked him in the eye and said, "Fuck you."

Then one of the guys sitting down said, "Hey listen, we don't want any trouble. Really, we're sorry."

"That's what I thought," I said. "A bunch of Goddamn pussies. Let's go, it stinks in here." We all three turned and went back to the hotel.

CHAPTER 27

Before leaving to go our separate ways, Alan, Randy, and I vowed to keep in closer contact than we had. We also made each other promise to call one of the others before we did anything like what David had done.

While on the plane for Thailand I began to think about Randy, and was becoming worried about him. Since leaving the service about four months earlier, he had been unable to find a job too. This didn't make sense because he was a bright man and had all the qualifications needed. Talking to Alan and me before we left, he told us of his frustrations in dealing with the world, and at one point said, "Maybe David had the right idea." I told him no, David didn't. And I reminded him that the four of us had vowed to make the deaths of the seven, who died so that we could live, count for something and not be forgotten.

A sadness crept through my body. Once again my emotions were at war with each other. My rage at the world was beginning to surface and I was ready to fight at the drop of a hat. My inability to get along with people began to drive me further into solitude. Linda and I once again began to argue. My final four months in Thailand were filled with one scrape after another and I wasn't coping well with anything. It was now time to return to the States and I knew things were going to get worse.

I received my orders and after a thirty day leave I was to be assigned to Fort Sill. My family left two weeks before I did. I was to meet them at her mother's where we would spend our leave. The day before I was to depart Colonel Myers sent word for me to report to him, and I did.

"John, before you leave I wanted to have a talk with you. Now this is strictly off the record and unofficial. I'm not talking to you as a commander but as someone that is concerned about you."

"Yes sir," I said.

"John, you've been through an experience that the civilian population can never comprehend. The civilians can't even imagine what the normal soldier goes through in Vietnam, and I think that every returning soldier is getting a bum rap. However, one of the reasons that we fight any war is for the basic rights and freedoms that our country affords us. These civilians have the right to say whatever they want about the war. I don't agree with them; in fact I think they're wrong, but they have the right."

"Sir, what you're saying is," I interrupted, "that they have the right to inflict mental cruelty to young men and cause these young men, who have honorably done their duty, as much mental pain as that Goddamn riceball who tortured me."

"No, I'm not. Nobody has the right to hurt others. I don't know how to explain it to you and I'm not justifying anyone's actions. However let me say this, you still have a lot of good in you. I understand the hard feelings you have to the Vietnamese and to the civilians, but that leaves you nowhere. You have so much hate building inside that unless you let go of that hate, its going to destroy you."

"Sir I have said time and time again, I have done nothing to be ashamed of and I don't think it's fair to ask me to give in and denounce my actions."

"I'm not asking you to do that. I don't think you get what I'm trying to tell you. The hate and anger you have is only going to hurt you, no one else. You don't have to give in to anyone, but don't allow the hate and anger to eat your insides and consume your life, it will destroy you. Just think about what I said, will you?"

"Yes sir I will, and thank you."

"Good luck John and keep in touch, ok?" He said shaking my hand.

He returned my salute in the same lax manner as he always had but this time with a smile. Soon I was on a plane bound for home. His words kept running through my head but I still didn't understand them. For some reason I couldn't help the hostile feelings I had.

After my leave was up I reported in at my next station. The commander there told me, "Captain I see in your file here, trouble. I want to assure you, I will not tolerate any misconduct at all. Is that clear?" I knew right away this was going to be tough duty.

Linda and I settled into a house just off post and she became very active with the other military wives. I began to crawl in a shell, not associating with anyone. I seldom ventured into public and very seldom associated with others on post. I grew intolerable of people and had to fight myself not to explode at them. I found haven only in drinking and sitting in solitude.

The first six months of my duty at Fort Sill went by without any major incidents. I wasn't getting into trouble but I was having a major conflict within myself. The mass of emotions were swelling inside me and had no outlet of escape. I held every emotion inside and would talk very little to anyone about anything.

One morning the commander called a formation of all troops. Everyone was assembled and the commander spoke to them, telling us that amnesty had been granted to all those who had evaded the draft. He said that if any of these evaders were to turn themselves in to any of us we were to take them immediately to HQ. None of us under any circumstances were to harm or in any other way do anything except take them to HQ. When the formation was dismissed the XO, Major Harris, heard me say, half under my breath, "I'd like to have one of those wimpy ass mothers turn himself into me."

"Captain Walker, do you understand the orders that were just given?"

"Yes sir." I responded in an angry tone gritting my teeth together.

"I don't think you do." The major said and proceeded to put me at attention and verbally reprimand me in front of everyone standing there.

Fury raced through my veins and suddenly I lost control. "You son of a bitch." I yelled as I swung my fist into his jaw and knocked him to the ground.

Two of the officers standing near by grabbed me, holding me from attacking him further. As the Major picked himself up from the ground he said, "Captain, you just got yourself a court martial." Then instructed the officers holding my arms to escort me to the commander's office.

I waited in the outer office for about fifteen minutes while the major briefed the commander on what had happened. Finally the Colonel's door opened and I was called in. "Captain what the hell is your problem?"

"I don't know sir."

"Well you better figure it out quick. The Major here will have a report of the charges on my desk first thing in the morning. As of this moment, Captain Walker you are under house arrest. That means you are to leave here, go home and not leave that location for any reason until I send for you. Is that clear Captain?"

"Yes sir."

CHAPTER 28

When I arrived home I told Linda what had happened. "What are they going to do?" She asked.

"I don't know. Probably court martial me. Who cares?"

The rest of the day I sat by myself, thinking of Colonel Myers' talk before I left Thailand. What was wrong with me? What was I becoming? I didn't want to feel the way I did nor did I want to act the way I did. Every time, after I pulled a stupid stunt like this I would be angry at myself. I knew better than that, so why does it happen? Why can't I control myself? Finally later that night, after drinking for most of it, I drifted off to sleep still asking why.

The next morning the colonel called me on the phone and told me to meet him at the Post Commander's office at fourteen hundred hours. I told him I would, hung up and thought to myself, "Boy, you have really screwed up this time."

When I arrived at the Post Commander's officer the Colonel was already there and they called me right in. "Captain Walker," The General said. "I have looked over your file and read these charges here. This doesn't appear to be the first time that you have struck another officer, does it?"

"No sir it isn't." I answered.

"Do you have an explanation or reason for this?"

"No sir, I don't."

"Do you realize the seriousness of these charges?"

"Yes sir, I do."

"You realize the seriousness of the charges but have nothing to say in your defense."

"That's correct sir." I said.

"Captain, from your records you were a good officer and received many accommodations. It looks like you started having trouble after being a POW, and that may be the root of your problems. Every effort has been made to help you and you haven't responded. And you damn sure aren't giving me much choice here. I hate to see your life ruined by a court martial so I am going to propose one alternative. You have until sixteen hundred hours tomorrow to request release from active duty, at which point these charges will be dropped. However, if you do not comply with this option I will have to court martial you. Do you understand?"

"Yes sir, I understand."

"Well, what are you going to do?" He asked.

"Sir, I'll probably request my release but I would like to talk it over with my wife."

"That's fine Captain. Here are the forms, take them home with you. Remember if you are going to submit them, have them here before sixteen hundred hours. That's all Captain, you're dismissed."

When I arrived home I told Linda what the General had said and she was totally in favor of getting out of the service. There was no discussion about staying in, it was almost an automatic decision. "How long before your release will become effective?" She asked.

"I don't know. I'll probably know tomorrow when I turn it in, but I don't imagine it'll take very long." I answered.

I was at the post commander's office before noon the next day with my request. I was told that it would only take two to three weeks to process and till then I was relieved of all duties.

On my return home I thought, "What now." I had no idea where to go from here. Linda and I had decided that we were returning to her home town, where we still owned a home. But what happens now? I knew that now I would be forced to deal with civilians and that worried me.

Once I arrived home I told Linda that I would be out of the service in two to three weeks and we needed to begin packing. I opened a beer and went to the phone. Alan had gotten out of the service a couple of months earlier and I decided to call. "Alan, how's civilian life?" I asked.

"Are you shitting me? These people are out in left field somewhere. How's everything with you?"

I told him what had happened and that I was being forced to get out. Alan asked what I planned to do and I told him I wasn't sure yet. He told me to call him when I was out, he might have something we could do together.

CHAPTER 29

For the first three months following my discharge from the military, I applied for a number of jobs flying. Each place that I applied would send me a nice letter saying thanks for my interest in their company but I just didn't have the experience that they were looking for. During this time I kept in contact with Alan and Randy. Randy, who upon his release from the military was unable to find employment, was working now as a soldier for hire. With the Vietnam War being in the final stages of the United States pulling out, there were still many rebellions throughout the world that needed people to quietly look after American interests. Randy was talking to Alan and me about going to work for this group that was involved in protecting American interests throughout the world. Alan and I weren't quite sure whether we wanted to join this group or not. "Who gives a shit about protecting these God Damn Americans?" I would say, however the money was awful damn good.

During the time following my discharge I worked at a number of jobs trying to make money. The jobs that I was able to get were in sales and on commission only. This type of job was extremely tough on me because I didn't get along with the public, still harboring ill feelings toward them. I remember when I got fired for almost punching out a customer while working as a car salesman. Car sales was an odd world because of the games they played. First getting a price that the customer will pay then getting a price the company will accept, then getting the customer to come up. I was with a couple one day trying to get them to raise the amount they would give and the husband was a real jerk. Somehow, I don't remember how or why exactly, Vietnam came up in our conversation. This guy was making a lot of derogatory statements about the war and the people who fought it. After listening to his repulsive comments and biting my tongue I could take no more. "Listen you wimpy ass bastard, I fought in Vietnam and I or the other men that served honorably there don't need or deserve your stupid ass comments and prejudices." I yelled across the desk at him.

The couple stood up and headed for the door as he said, "I don't believe I wish to do any business with a barbarian that would support the atrocities committed in Vietnam."

They were already on the show room floor before he finished his statement and I was coming from behind the desk with fire in my eyes. The sales manager had already been alerted to the situation and had a couple of other salesmen with him. The three of them intervened getting between us keeping me from smashing the guys face. The sales manager tried to smooth things with the couple and keep them from leaving but was unsuccessful. Then he turned to me telling me to get my things and get out.

Similar events took place in all the short term jobs I was able to get. Linda and I began to have arguments about my inability to retain employment. We grew further and further apart as she began to live in the world of her friends and seeing "Uncle Bill". The work that Randy was doing began to look more and more attractive. Finally Alan and I agreed to meet Randy and a representative of the group in Dallas.

When we arrived in Dallas we were put up in one of the nicer hotels and only had to sign for whatever we wanted. "Damn I could get used to this pretty easy." Alan said and I agreed. The day after we arrived Alan and I were picked up by Randy and driven to a large estate on the out skirts of town. Randy explained that this place would house about ten to twelve people and was one of many throughout the country used as a safe haven by the group for people when not on missions. Randy led us past a living area where several people were watching TV, to a large den in the back. "You guys want a drink?" Randy asked.

"Yeah, sure." We answered.

"The man that's going to tell you all about things will be down in just a minute." Randy told us as he handed us our drinks.

In the middle of a sip of my drink I almost choked when the tall, slightly graying representative entered the room. "How are you John?" He asked.

"Fine sir." I responded still somewhat choking.

"I guess you're surprised to see me, uh."

"Yes Colonel Myers, I am."

CHAPTER 30

When Alan and I arrived back at the hotel my mind was still pondering everything that Colonel Myers had told us. The colonel was a true patriot, retiring from the military to continue fighting for the American cause. He had been subjected to the same contempt and scorn from the American public as I had, but he still believed in them. Even though the public condemned us for what we as a country must do, those things had to have been done in order to keep America a free nation. Although I still had many ill feelings, I knew that what he said was true: the United States still was and is the greatest nation on earth.

"What do you think?" I asked Alan as I took a long drink from my scotch that had been delivered by room service.

"Well, it could be some tough duty, but the money sure sounds good."

"Yeah, and I sure can use the money."

"Me too. What do you think the wives will say? You know he said we would be gone a couple, three months at a time."

I took a deep breath then a pull from my cigarette, "I don't think it matters to Linda. She'd probably just as soon not have me around anyway," I answered.

"Yeah, I'm in the same boat, John."

"Ya know, I think we can do it all right. He said that we could be on the same team together."

"Are you kidding? With us together we could do anything," Alan said with a chuckle.

"Yeah," I replied with a grin. "I think we ought to call Randy in the morning and have him tell Myers we're in."

"Yeah, I agree, but it's already morning. Let's call now." Alan said as we both looked at our watches, seeing that it was four-twenty A.M.

As I reached for the phone an excitement began to build inside me. Maybe this is what Alan and I needed to bring us back to the land of the living, I thought. I dialed the number that Randy had given us and asked to speak to him.

"Hey, Randy, this is John. Did I wake you?"

"Are you shitting me? We're still partying here."

"God damn, you guys really are tough. Hey listen, Alan and I have decided to go in."

Randy cut me off before I could finish my statement, "We don't talk about anything on the phone, but I think that's great. Hey, you guys got a rental car, do you think you can find your way over here?"

"Yeah, I guess so. Why?"

"You guys jump in the car and drive over, we're going to be partying for a long time yet. The man is upstairs asleep so you will be here when he gets up and that way you can tell him yourselves."

"Jesus Christ, Randy, it's almost five o'clock in the morning. Don't you guys ever sleep?"

"Don't worry about sleep, if you're tired I got something that'll keep you awake. Just jump in the car and get over here. Ok?"

"What the hell. We're on our way."

I sat the receiver down and shaking my head told Alan everything Randy had said. Alan smiled and said, "Damn, this could turn out to be fun duty."

I agreed, and with wide grins we left the room.

The sun was beginning to peek over the horizon when we reached the house that we had left only hours earlier. Randy almost dragged us into the house and began introductions. "Hey guys, this is the two I told you about. They're part of us now."

Everyone gathered around, shook our hands and gave their names. As one shoved a drink into our hands he said, "I hear that you two are some tough mother fuckers."

With a grin and a shrug of modesty Alan stated, "Whoever told you that must be drunk," and everyone laughed.

"I'm not drunk yet," Randy yelled out as he handed us a small mirror with lines of cocaine evenly drawn. "Here, take a snort of this, it'll pick you right up."

After a few hours of war stories, booze, and drugs, Colonel Myers emerged from his slumber. "I don't suppose anyone is drinking any coffee yet," he stated with a laugh. "And since you all have two extra partiers I hope it means what I think it means."

"I think it does, sir," I said.

"Good. Let me make some coffee, since this old man needs it first thing in the morning, then I'll talk with you."

About fifteen minutes later he reappeared holding a mug of coffee, and told us to come with him. We followed him down the hall to the only locked room in the house. It was like an enormous study, with a large wooden desk and an overstuffed couch. He had us sit on the couch as he took his place behind the desk. "You boys decided pretty quick, didn't you?"

"Yes sir," I answered.

"Well I like that, but you understand what you're getting into, don't you?"

"Yes sir, I think so," I said as Alan was nodding his head in concurrence.

"You know it gets awfully tough out there sometimes."

"Sir, I don't think anything can be as bad as what we've already been through," Alan stated.

"No, I guess not," he said with a smile. "All right, you're in and I'm mighty glad to have you."

"Thank you, sir," we both said as he was scribbling something on a pad.

Handing us what he had just written down and while unlocking his desk drawer he said, "Be at that address in Miami on the twenty-fifth. That will give you about three weeks to take care of any personal matters you may have." Taking out two envelopes from the drawer he had just unlocked, he added, "Here is five thousand dollars each to help you out. I'll meet you in Miami and explain everything then. Any questions?"

"No sir," we both answered, half in shock at the suddenness of everything.

"Ok. Once again it's good to have you with us," he said shaking our hands and walking us out the door.

In the car on the way back to the hotel I said, "Damn, these people move fast."

"No shit!" Alan answered.

"I can't believe this. We said before we came down here we weren't going to make any quick decisions."

"Yeah, but we climbed aboard so now we have to make the best of it."

"Yeah, it's too late to back track now," I said with a smile.

"Let's meet in Miami on the twenty-second and take a couple of days to look around, ok?"

"Sounds good to me pal."

CHAPTER 31

Arriving home in the early evening, I discovered a baby sitter at the house with the boys. When she told me that Linda was out for the evening, I knew that Linda was probably out with "Uncle Bill". At first I thought about going out bar hopping myself and maybe running into them, but rejected the idea. I told the young girl that we wouldn't need her to stay as I would be home with the boys and paid her what Linda normally paid her.

I let the boys stay up for an hour past their bedtime so we could watch TV and play games. I wanted to spend as much time as I could with them over the next two weeks, not knowing what my new job would bring.

After the boys fell asleep on the sofa watching TV, I carried them off to bed and tucked them in. Then opening a beer I sat out on the back patio, letting my mind wander. "Why do things happen the way they do?" I asked myself. I wondered what Linda and Bill were doing and how I should or would react when she returned home. Was I such an evil person that I didn't deserve some happiness also? These questions and many more went through my mind as I finished off a six-pack of beer. I could find no answers. I felt upset at my feelings of jealousy and wanted to run away right then, but knew I could not leave the boys alone. I had no right to begrudge Linda the happiness that I had failed to provide her, but I thought I still loved her, or was it that I wanted some happiness too?

After getting another beer from the refrigerator I again reclined in the lounge chair on the patio. The tiny little spots of glitter sparkling across the black sky seemed to be in perfect harmony with the singing of the crickets and the cool breeze that caressed my face. How tranquil and peaceful the heavens must be. Why couldn't I find some of that tranquility here on earth, I wondered. Searching the stars for the answers to my questions I slipped into a light slumber.

When I awoke, the blackness of night was beginning to gray and I knew that the sun would soon be climbing in the sky. I looked at my watch. It was five-thirty in the morning and wondered if Linda had returned home while I was asleep. I stood up, reaching my arms to the sky to stretch my muscles, and then walked into the bedroom. Linda had not returned home and a sorrow passed through my being. Suddenly I knew that our life together was doomed to fail and that I was at fault.

After taking a quick shower I brewed a pot of coffee. As I sat at the kitchen table savoring the brew I had made, I heard a car pull up and knew Linda was finally returning. When she walked through the front door and saw me at the kitchen table a look of sudden terror crossed her face.

"When did you get home?" She asked in a squeaky, fearful voice.

"Yesterday."

"Where are the boys?"

"They're still in bed. What time do they have to go to school?"

"Eight o'clock, but they need to get up about now so they can eat before they go," she said, still afraid and somewhat confused at my calmness.

"I'll get them up," I said.

Linda nervously fixed them breakfast and dressed them. Once they were prepared for school I said, "I'll drive them."

"Ok. Are you coming right back?" She asked, still avoiding any eye contact with me.

"I don't know. Why?"

"Because I think we need to talk."

"Yeah. I guess so. I'll be back in a few minutes."

As I drove back to the house my mind muddled through the topic that was to be discussed when I returned home. I knew it was best if I just moved out of the house and besides in a couple of weeks I would be gone anyway.

When I arrived home Linda was just getting out of the shower and had a towel wrapped around her. "I'm sorry John."

"Don't be," I said pouring myself a cup of coffee. "I'm going to move my things out today and I'll check into a hotel."

Tears began to stream down her face. "That's not what I want, John."

"What do you mean, that's not what you want? What do you want?"

"I don't know. I'm so confused."

"Look, I know I've put you through hell and I'm sorry. I also know I'm not the same person I used to be. I wish I was. Anyway I took a job which starts in a couple of weeks. I'll be gone for a couple, three months at a time."

"What kind of job is it?"

"I'll be flying again."

"For who?"

"It's a company that flies overseas." I tried to be evasive about who it was.

"Oh, John, we have to work things out. Let's try. Ok?"

"Linda, you are really confusing me."

"I know, I'm confused too," she said as she put her arms around my neck and kissed me.

Over the next week my emotions were at conflict with themselves. I doubted her but didn't want to. I was angry with her but loved her. I wanted to leave her but needed someone to care about me. There was no end to the mixed feelings I had. Maybe she was right, we needed to work things out, and that's what I chose to do.

CHAPTER 32

Alan and I met in Miami on the twenty-second and found a hotel in the Coral Gables area, close to the address we were to report to. We spent the next two days basking in the sun and touring a few of the many sights that Miami offered. On the morning of the twenty-fifth we checked out of the hotel and took a taxi to the address we were given.

We were greeted at the door by a husky young man who led us to a lounging area. Telling us to make ourselves at home and quickly disappeared.

"Good morning, gentlemen. How are you today?" Colonel Myers greeted us, holding out his hand. "This is General Gibbons, United States Air Force, retired," he said, introducing the man who was with him.

General Gibbons was a gray haired, well preserved combatant of World War II. He had been retired from the Air Force for seventeen years and had been active all that time with this organization. He was involved with the organizing of Air America and still served as an advisor to the United Nations. At the age of seventy-four, the General still had the mind of a forty year old. His uncanny ability to analyze enemy objectives made him an expert strategist. "The colonel here has told me about you two, and for the most part I like what I've heard," he said in a gravelly voice.

"Thank you, sir," we answered.

"I respect the sacrifice you have made and I admire your courage and toughness. However, I think you need to get over flying off the handle. You see, boys, I have dedicated my entire adult life to keeping this country the great nation that it is, and sometimes the people of this country go against what is in their best interest. People like myself must do the dirty work that allows them the freedom to denounce us and we can't let that get under our skin."

Alan and I both stated that we understood. Colonel Myers was shuffling through some papers to reveal a map and asked, "Can you guys estimate about where you were imprisoned here on the map?"

"We were asked that several times in our debriefing," Alan began. "As far as we figured the camp was about here," Alan was pointing to a spot in Laos.

"I think that's about it," I said. "It only took a day's march to reach the main trail which we believe was the Ho Chi Minh Trail. Why is it important?"

"Because," General Gibbons paused to light his pipe. "The North Vietnamese are already taking over South Vietnam and probably preparing to go into Cambodia. Our intelligence tells us that they are using this area, here about where you were, as a staging area."

"I thought that we were out of all that now," I commented.

"Son we are, officially," the general said as he puffed on his pipe. "But it's like I said earlier. The public wanted us out so we got out. However the public doesn't always know what's best. This organization is involved in many covert actions that the public doesn't know about and of course we want to keep it that way."

Colonel Myers took over, "These covert actions are vital to our country and because of the way we conduct them it gives our government deniability to protect them from embarrassment. Now you two are going to be on a team with four other people and if on any mission you are caught or anything else, your employment and even existence will be totally denied."

"You mean if something ever happens that we're just flat-ass out on our own?" Alan asked.

"Not quite. You'll find that we take very good care of our people. However we will not acknowledge that you work for us, but quietly we will do everything to aid you. You understand what I'm saying?"

We answered the colonel by saying, "I think so."

General Gibbons interjected, "This is going to be about the last chance you have to back out. You want out?"

"No sir. I guess every job has some risk to it," Alan answered, speaking for both of us.

"Good," Colonel Myers said. "We'll have a briefing right here in this room at o-nine-hundred hours tomorrow. At that time you'll meet the other four and learn about your first mission. The rest of today you're free to do what you want. You can hang around here, these facilities are for your use, or go downtown if you like. You both have a room upstairs; just take one that isn't in use. One thing that I want to emphasize, though. Everything that is said in here is top secret and is not to be repeated at all. You don't even talk about it between yourselves outside of this house. Is that understood?"

"Yes sir," we answered.

"Good." Colonel Myers' expression relaxed from the stern look to a smile, as all four of us stood up. Then holding out his hand, "welcome aboard."

The house seemed to have everything. After we put our bags in two empty rooms upstairs we began to explore. There was a big screen TV with VCR in the living room and a pool table and ping pong table in the den. The bar was stocked with a more than ample supply of beer and liquor. The patio and swimming pool in the back yard were completely enclosed by a ten foot high cinderblock wall. There was no doubt, this house was as luxurious as the one we were at in Dallas.

That afternoon several others arrived at the house. We all introduced ourselves, but no one spoke about what they were doing there. Alan and I played pool, drank, swam, drank, watched TV, and drank some more 'till early evening.

I woke early the next morning and lay quietly, allowing my thoughts to drift through my head. I thought of Linda and the boys and wondered what she was doing. I told myself that I would call them this afternoon. I wondered what this job would bring and why they asked the questions about where we were held captive. A knock at my door broke the pattern of my thoughts.

"Yeah," I yelled.

As the door opened Alan said, "How about us getting something to eat before the briefing?"

"Sounds good to me," I said as I slung my feet over the edge of the bed. "I got to shower yet, though."

"Yeah, me too. I'll meet you downstairs in about fifteen minutes."

"Ok."

Alan and I returned from breakfast about fifteen before nine and went straight to the briefing room. Colonel Myers was already there, along with four others when we walked in he stood, saying, "John, Alan, good morning. Let me introduce you. This is A.J. He is the team leader."

"Good to meet you sir," I said.

"Don't have to call me sir. Welcome aboard. Colonel Myers has told me a lot about you."

"Hope some of it has been good," Alan answered.

Everyone chuckled as we shook hands and were introduced to the others.

General Gibbons entered the room and said, "Everyone's here. Good. Let's get down to business." He was a very serious type of person and very seldom smiled. I wondered if he was an unhappy person or just very businesslike in front of us.

Pulling a map down that was rolled on the wall, "Men, I'm sure you recognize this map. A.J. here has already been briefed and will give you more details later. As you already know, we believe that North Vietnam is trying to take over Cambodia. They're using this area here in Laos as a staging area. We're sure they have a munitions depot about here and a troop training area about here. Your job is to map this area and destroy the munitions depot. Now you're not going to have a lot of time to train for this one. You'll be taken to the training area in the morning and only have about three weeks to plan everything out. Does anyone have any questions?"

As Colonel Myers sensed what my bewildered look was saying he spoke up, "A.J. will have the specific objectives, time table, and maps. He'll have a detailed briefing at the training site. Now then, the van will leave here in the morning at o-seven-hundred hours to take you to the training area, and since the general and I have a plane to catch that's it for this briefing. I'll see you all in a couple of weeks and until then, good luck."

127

CHAPTER 33

The van ride to the training area took a little over an hour, and the ride was made with almost no conversation. As we arrived at the site the early morning ball of fire in the sky had already begun to push the temperature upwards and the humidity hung like an invisible cloud of vapor. The emerald tropic vegetation glowed with the morning rays of the sun as the animals sang reveille to the world. I thought how deceiving the jungle could be. In appearance it was so peaceful and beautiful, seeming to be in perfect harmony with nature, but it could be a cruel and savage place in reality.

Unloading our bags at the small wooden frame building where we stopped, A.J. said, "Grab a room and put your things away. We'll have a briefing in thirty minutes."

A.J. was a stocky guy about five foot nine with sandy blond hair. He was an ex Special Forces officer and like the rest of us had served a couple tours in Vietnam. I thought how typical he was of all the Special Forces guys that I had known in Thailand.

Since none of us had much to put away, we all sat around drinking coffee and talking about Vietnam while we waited for the briefing. I couldn't help but wonder what we were in for and how it all would turn out.

A.J. entered the room and hung several maps on the wall. He began the briefing by saying we were to land in Bangkok where we would pick up a LOCH (Huges 500 helicopter) and all the armament we needed for the mission. From that point on we would be on our own and could not expect any help from anyone including the Thai government. We would proceed to a village, which we called Point Alpha, which was close to the Laos border. Hiding the helicopter in the jungle, we would proceed by foot to try and find the munitions depot and troop training area. "We don't know the exact location of these installations because the overgrowth is so dense they can't be spotted by air. However our best estimate is they're about here."

As A.J. pointed to a spot on the map I spoke up, "A.J. forgive me, but I'm new to this and I've got a question."

"Go ahead. What is it?"

"Well it seems to me that a march from point alpha to that area is going to be a good three day march at a fast pace. Since we want to get in and out as fast as possible, why don't we fly into here?" I asked, pointing to another spot on the map. "There used to be a Special Forces helipad there."

"Do you know the exact location and can you land there at night?"

"I've flown in there several times when I was flying for Myers. Landing at night, though, might be another matter."

"I know the pad he's talking about, I've been in there many times," Doug said. "Since the exit time is more critical, why not have me and maybe Skip walk in from point alpha to there and carry a couple bean bag lights?"

"John, you think you can land there with a couple bean bags?" A.J. asked.

"Sure. I don't see why I couldn't?"

Over the next two weeks every detail was planned to the minute. I was impressed with the thoroughness of the plans. Every contingency was planned for and each plan had a backup plan. Each person on the team had a special expertise but was completely trained and knowledgeable in all areas. During the day we would rehearse the different tasks of the mission to get the exact timing, then at night we would make adjustments. Nothing was left to chance.

Colonel Myers walked into the briefing room in his normal easy gait. His arrival was not unexpected, as he had told us in Miami he would see us in a couple of weeks so we were expecting him. "Good evening, gentlemen," he expressed. "How's the planning coming along?"

"Fine," A.J. answered. "We're ready."

"Good. How's the two new men doing?" He asked A.J., nodding his head toward Alan and me, and then stood smiling at us.

Neither Alan nor I had ever asked what had happened to the two that we replaced. We didn't think they would tell us and besides, we probably didn't want to know.

"I think they're going to work out real fine sir," A.J. answered.

"Great. You got the plan worked out?"

"Yes sir. I think we can be ready to go any time now."

"That's terrific. You all can brief me tonight and tomorrow, and I'll give you the details of getting you to Bangkok. Gentlemen, we leave for Bangkok day after tomorrow."

CHAPTER 34

We were accompanied on the commercial flight to Bangkok by Colonel Myers. Landing there late at night we were met by security and whisked away without going through customs. Security took us to the opposite side of the airport, which was the Air Force MAC V headquarters, to a secured hanger. Once there, our plan went into effect. Each one of us undressed, donned jungle fatigues and quickly went about our assigned tasks of checking the gear, armament, and rations, and then loading it on the aircraft. Each man worked individually and together like a well made Swiss watch. Soon A.J. announced to Colonel Myers, "We're ready to leave sir."

"Well, gentlemen, this is where I leave you. From now on you're on your own. I wish you good luck and my prayers go with you, and I buy the first round when you return. All right, open the hanger doors and head out."

We quickly rolled the helicopter out of the hanger and everyone boarded the aircraft. I started the bird and radioed the tower, "Tower, this is special flight bravo one. Request immediate takeoff from MAC V pad to the west, over."

As I pulled the bird to a hover I could see Colonel Myers still standing by the hanger giving us thumbs up. I nodded my head and smiled, then off we went.

Alan, sitting in the co-pilot's seat, pulled out the maps to navigate with and gave me the first heading. I turned the aircraft to a heading of zero-eight-zero degrees as Alan lit a cigarette and handed it to me.

"Thanks."

"Don't mention it."

"Alan, let me know when we're fifteen minutes out," A.J. said.

"Roger."

The full moon lit up the sky like a giant searchlight and made navigation easy. The air was calm and made the flight smooth as if we were gliding on a sheet of glass. I made the last heading change and Alan announced, "A.J. we're fifteen out."

"Roger."

The scurrying of the men behind me, to get securely fastened in, touched off the butterflies in my stomach. Knowing that night landings in the jungle with lighted pads were sometimes tough and we were now going to land with no lights except for the light of the moon. A.J. asked, "Can you see well enough, John?"

"Sure. This one's a cinch compared to the next one we have to make."

"Are you kidding? This guy could land anything, anywhere, with his eyes closed," Alan stated with a semi-tense chuckle.

I turned my head and said, "Right."

"Let's not make Alan out a liar, ok?" A.J. said with a smirk.

"There's the landing site right over there. You got it?" Alan said as he pointed to it.

"Yeah, I got it," I replied as I began the approach.

"All right, if you need any help let me know and I'll open my eyes," Alan laughed.

"Thanks a lot."

I brought the helicopter to a stop on the ground and shut off the engine. Swiftly everyone exited the aircraft and set about their tasks. Alan and I began to tie the chopper down while A.J. and Larry unfolded the camouflage netting to hide the bird. Doug and Skip were preparing for their march to point bravo where we would hide the bird while we went in on the mission. Soon the helicopter was secured and completely hidden. Doug and Skip were ready to depart.

"Alright you two have to be in position by tomorrow night," A.J. told Doug and Skip.

"We'll be there."

"Now, we'll time it to be there between twenty-three hundred hours and twenty-three-ten. You have the bean bags on during that time only. If we're not there by twenty-three-ten go to plan B. Ok?"

"No problem, A.J. we'll see you guys later," Doug announced as they headed into the jungle.

When first light broke through the darkness we found the two fifty-gallon drums of fuel that had been stashed there, by whom I did not know. It took all four of us to roll the drums to the aircraft, then while the other three arranged our gear I refueled the bird with a hand pump. By nightfall everything was organized and all that was left to do the next day was some last minute planning for the second leg of our mission.

When twilight came the next evening all preparations had been checked and rechecked. As we prepared to unmask the chopper I made my last minute flight calculations.

"Alright A.J., here's what I got," I said as I unfolded my map to brief A.J. "I figure the flight in is going to take an hour and twenty minutes, not factoring in any winds aloft. The best calculation that I can come up with is that we'll have a headwind or quartering headwind of about fifteen to twenty knots. That's going to add about sixteen to eighteen minutes to the flight. Now what I've come up with is if we depart here at twenty-one-twenty that will give us an hour forty for the flight. If we're early we can circle here at this spot; that's far enough away not to call attention to point bravo but close enough that we can make it within the ten minutes."

"Looks good, John," A.J. commented, pressing his lips together and nodding his head. "Alright everyone, let's uncover and get ready. We leave at twenty-one-twenty."

CHAPTER 35

Darkness had settled in and a thin cloud cover gave us less light than we had two nights before. Lifting off exactly at twenty-one-twenty hours, I wondered about how much light there would be at point bravo. Not having any navigational aids to fly by, I had to fly by the time and distance method. Alan once again was in the co-pilot's seat doing most of the navigation.

"How we looking?" A.J. asked, as he leaned between the cockpit seats.

"We're about right here," Alan answered, pointing to a spot on the map. "And right now it's twenty-two-fifty."

"It looks like we'll arrive at about twenty-three-o-five," I said.

"Great," A.J. answered. "Any problems with landing being it's this dark?"

"No, I don't think so. As long as I can get those bean bags in sight. But when I start the approach you guys can open the back doors and keep me clear on the sides," I stated.

"No problem. Just tell us when."

"We should be coming up on point bravo anytime now," Alan announced.

"There they are, at about two o'clock," came A.J.'s words.

"I got 'em," I said, as I turned the aircraft to the right, heading directly for the little lights. "God damn, that area looks small."

"Ain't no problem for you. Is it?" Alan said with a half laugh.

As I began my descent I said, "All right, open those doors. As soon as the tail rotor clears the trees, let me know."

"Roger."

I eased the helicopter into what seemed like a small hole in the foliage. As soon as the skids touched the ground I shut down the engine and Doug and Skip ran up to the bird. Once again everyone knew what their task was and set about doing it. In less than fifteen minutes the helicopter was hidden under the camouflage net and all our provisions ready to go.

Slinging our packs to our backs A.J. said, "Alright let's hit it," and off into the jungle we went.

The night air was cool as my mind drifted back to the last time I had walked through the jungle. This march seemed like a cakewalk compared to that last one when four of us went in search of our freedom.

When the light of day began to creep up on the darkness, we nestled into a thick clump of overgrowth. Unfolding his map A.J. said, "Alright, we're about here. The munitions depot should be over here and the troop training area about here. We'll use this as a base here and dig our gear in. As in our plan we'll break up into three two-man recon teams. Alan, you and John take this area and Doug, you and Skip take this one, Larry and I will take this one. Now we'll meet back here at nineteen hundred hours tonight. Any questions?" With no one having any questions A.J. said, "Well then, let's get it on." We quickly hid all our gear and the teams scampered to their assigned areas.

As the sun climbed high in the sky so did the temperature, and sweat began to saturate my jungle fatigues. We moved swiftly but cautiously through our area making notes of everything that might be important.

"Alan," I whispered, "looks like a trail over there."

"Yeah, and a big one too. Let's check it out."

The path was as wide as a one-lane road and Alan said, "Looks like it's used a lot, don't it?"

"Yeah. Let's see where it goes."

Alertly, we crept along the trail ready for anything that might happen. Soon we could see an open area in which the trail seemed to lead. Deciding it would be best to explore the open area from some place other than the trail, we reentered the jungle and edged our way to the opening. Taking our field glasses from their cases, we began to survey the area. There were a number of people working in the rice field and beyond them was a camp of what appeared to be soldiers.

"Ya think this is the troop training area?" I asked.

"It sure looks like it," Alan replied. "How many you make there is?"

"There's at least two, maybe three hundred."

"Yeah, and looks like they've got plenty of armament, too."

"Wait a minute, Alan! Those aren't villagers!" My voice cracked and I shuddered while my mind recounted my days of imprisonment. "They're Americans, Alan!"

"Sure as hell looks that way," Alan's voice was strained also.

"Those riceballs are using our people for slave labor."

"Yeah. I count about fourteen guards around them. Let's move around to the north side there and maybe we can get a better look."

Alan and I spent the next three and a half hours mapping every detail of the area. We recorded approximate distances, buildings, storage areas, fences, everything. Not one item went unrecorded. Then Alan said, "It's almost sixteen hundred hours, we'd better get moving or we'll be late."

"Yeah," I said as we began our walk back to where we all were to meet.

CHAPTER 36

Once back at our rendezvous point, everyone made their reports. Doug and Skip had made a detailed recon of the munitions depot and it looked like it would be harder to destroy than we had first thought. When Alan and I told about the troop area and that there were Americans there A.J. said, "You made a detailed sketch of the whole area, didn't you?"

"Yeah, it's a pretty big area, but we got it all," Alan said.

"Good. Now about this depot," A.J. was saying when I interrupted him.

"What are we going to do about those Americans?" I asked.

A.J. looked at me, pressed his lips together, then looking back at the map and shaking his head, said, "Nothing we can do, John."

"What do you mean, nothing we can do? God damn it A.J., those are Americans, being used as slave labor and I know what it's like to be imprisoned by those riceballs," I blurted out.

"Jesus Christ, John, there ain't anything we can do. We have our orders and even if we broke the orders how the hell we going to get them out? First of all, there are only six of us against two or three hundred gooks and second, there ain't any room in the helicopter. Now I'd love to do something, but we can't and we're going by the orders."

I started to object when Alan put his hand on my shoulder and said, "John, I feel as bad as you do about not doing anything for those guys, but we both know A.J. is right. It's not going to do anyone any good for us all to get killed and not accomplish the mission. I'm sure Myers will give us the opportunity to come back and get them."

"Yeah, you're right. It's just that I hate to leave anyone under those riceballs control," I said.

"I know," A.J. said. "I wish there was something we could do but there isn't. But there is something we can do about this depot and we need to figure something out fast."

Darkness had completely surrounded us by the time we had adapted our plan. We uncovered our packs and headed for objective. It took a little over two hours to reach the depot, and before we went in we once again reviewed everyone's assignment. It took each of us about forty-five minutes to crawl to our assigned targets and carefully place an explosive charge. We set each charge to detonate in two hours so we would have a little over an hour's head start for the helicopter and would probably need every second of it.

Once all the charges were in place and we had all joined up, A.J. said, "Alright let's get the hell out of here!" And we swiftly began our journey to the helicopter. We knew that once the charges went off they would have the jungle full of soldiers looking for us.

After rushing through the jungle for a little over an hour we heard the thunderous explosion of our work and could see the light of our deed above the trees. Not even taking time to savor the moment, we picked up our pace as there were still about five hours left in the race to the chopper.

The sun had already begun to wake the jungle animals when we arrived at the helicopter. For about the last hour we could hear someone behind us and knew they were on our trail and not far behind. As Alan and A.J. were quickly stripping the camouflage net off the aircraft I started the engine and the others threw our gear inside. I brought the RPM up to operating speed and everyone boarded as I lifted the aircraft from the ground.

As we sped away at tree top level everyone sighed in relief. We had accomplished our mission without a shot ever being fired and soon we would be in Bangkok, then the U.S.

My mind quickly thought of the imprisoned Americans left behind. As I looked at Alan, I knew he was thinking the same and he said, "We'll come back for them."

I pressed my lips together and nodded, "Yep. We will."

CHAPTER 37

"Dong Mong Tower, this is bravo one, five miles northeast, request landing instructions for MAC V. Over."

"Bravo One, you're cleared to MAC V pad direct. Winds are one-seven-zero, altimeter two-niner-niner-two."

"Bravo one, roger," I responded as I lined the helicopter up for my final approach.

I brought the bird to a hover, then gently set it down. Immediately, security guards encircled the aircraft and quickly we rolled the helicopter inside the secured hanger. Once inside, we quickly washed and changed to our street clothes and were given our airline tickets to return to the United States on a flight that was to leave in two and a half hours. Again security joined us and provided an escort to the civilian side of the airport. Once more we were not required to pass through customs or any screening.

On the plane I sat quietly, with my mind not on the mission we had just flawlessly completed, but on the Americans left behind. Projections of the savagery and tortures I had undergone flashed across my mind. I wondered if after all these years in captivity these men were anything but mere animals now and if they could ever fit back into society again. I wished I could have talked to them and told them we would be back for them, at least giving them some hope.

I turned to Alan sitting next to me, and knew he was also thinking as I was. "You think we can get them out?" I asked.

"It's going to take a damn good plan," he responded. "But we mapped it out real good and we should be able to come up with something."

A.J. leaned over the seat in front of us and said, "Look, you guys, I know how you feel about those guys back there and I'm really sorry there wasn't something we could've done."

"We understand," I said.

"There's one thing I want you to understand," A.J. continued. "The six of us are a team now and what affects one effect all. I think if all of us approach Myers with this he'll give us the backing to go back, and we all go in as a team. Ok?"

"Ok, and thanks, A.J.," Alan said with a sad smile.

Our flight landed in New York where we were met by an agent who cleared us through customs. We were then taken by private plane to Miami where we were taken by limousine to the safe house.

Colonel Myers was waiting for us and as we entered the room he shook each of our hands and said, "Great job."

"Colonel Myers," I started, "we've got something we need to tell you about that place."

"A.J. can brief me on all that later," he interrupted me, "but right now I've got some bad news, I'm sorry to say. I don't know any easy way to say this so I'll just come out with it. Randy is dead."

The news slammed through my head like the rifle butts used to slam into my face. A sudden panic flashed through my body as they helped Alan and me to the couch to sit down. Alan's face was ghostly white as he sat, unable to even speak. "What happened?" I managed to ask, as Colonel Myers handed Alan and me a hefty glass of scotch.

I took a long pull of the scotch as Colonel Myers said, "I don't know all the facts yet, but it looks like he committed suicide."

"Oh my God, no!" Bellowed Alan, dropping his glass as he began to sob.

Fighting back the tears, I stood on my weakened legs and set my drink down as I stumbled toward Alan. I put my hand on his shoulder, and not being able to hold back my tears I looked skyward as Colonel Myers said, "I want you two to rest here for a while then I have a plane standing by to take you to Dallas."

CHAPTER 38

Neither Alan nor I spoke a word on the flight to Dallas. No words were needed to express the deep sorrow that we both felt. Even though we both searched for answers we knew there were none.

When we arrived in Dallas there was a car waiting to take us to the Dallas safe house. As I entered the house, I thought back to when we joined the agency and partied with Randy right here. Everyone expressed their condolences and asked if there was anything they could do. We said there wasn't and thanked them.

I thought I'd better call Linda and tell her what was going on and that I would be home in a few days.

"Hello."

"Hey baby, it's me. How you doing?" I asked.

"John." She had a startled sound to her voice. "Where are you?"

"I'm in Dallas. I'll be here for a couple more days then be home."

Before I could tell her about Randy she said, "John, before you come here I need to tell you something."

"What?"

"Well, week before last I filed for a divorce. Oh, John, I'm sorry but I just don't think it will work out. Ya know what I mean?"

"Yeah," I said, trying not to show any emotion, but feeling as if the whole world was coming down around me. "I understand. I'll call you in a few days and work everything out."

"John, I'm sorry to ask but do you think you could send the boys some money?"

"Yeah. I'll send it right away. Talk to you later," and hung up.

I went up to Alan's room where he was lying on his bed, staring at the ceiling. I told him what Linda had just said and he reacted, "Huh. I wonder if she's been talking to Barbara. I can't even find her."

"What the hell's happening, Alan?"

"I don't know, pal."

We sat up all night talking, drinking and snorting cocaine. We remembered everything about David, Randy, the POW camp, our escape, and life back here in the States. The next day we went to Randy's funeral then returned to the house and drank ourselves into a stupor.

The morning after the funeral we sat drinking coffee, each with a massive hangover. "What happens now?" I asked.

"I don't know," Alan responded. "I guess life goes on."

"I wonder why sometimes."

"Me too, pal."

"Alan, promise me that you'll never take this way out."

"I don't know if I want to make that promise, John."

"Goddamn it Alan, I don't think I could take it. When we go, we go out together. Ok?"

"Ok, pal. But right now we got a job to do. Let's call Myers and get those guys out. What do you say?"

"Let's go" I responded. "Let's get it on."

CHAPTER 39

Aboard the plane carrying us back to Miami, my mind began to sift through the scrambled thoughts in my head. I thought of how elated David, Randy, Alan and I were when we escaped from the POW camp, then the collapse of that elation as we tried to cope with our own private hells here at home. I wondered if Alan and I were destined for one more final escape just as David and Randy made their final escape.

My mind shifted to the Americans left behind in Vietnam. I wondered if any of them were in the camp we had endured and had escaped from years ago and what they must be going through. They must be mere shells of men by now and completely convinced that we have forsaken them. Were they right? Had our government merely written them off to forget the war? How could a great and powerful nation discard the ones that so dutifully obeyed and carried out the missions it deemed necessary to preserve freedom in the world? I remembered the clichés "Freedom has a price", "Many good men have paid the price so we could live free", "Our forefathers had shed their blood so we could be free today". However, all these phrases have no meaning if we as a whole aren't thankful for the sacrifices made. If the people aren't willing to acknowledge and stand behind the men that made the ultimate sacrifice of all, what good is freedom?

My thoughts drifted to a western I had once seen on TV. The people of a small town had been terrorized and dictated to by a rich cattle baron. He ran the town, owned the law and got anything he wanted. The good people of the town wanted a freedom they could never have as long as this rancher was in rule of the town. However, these good people were afraid of losing their lives should they stand up to or cross this rancher. Therefore they merely survived in a hostile environment only dreaming of a better life.

Then one day a young man rides into town seemingly unafraid of anything. He's fast on the draw and is willing to stand up for himself and what he feels is right. The young man stands against a group of the rancher's men over a saloon girl. He out draws one of the men, the rest back down and leave. All of a sudden the good town's people think he is the one to lead them to the land of milk and honey that they dream of. The mayor approaches the young man, buys him a drink and offers him anything and everything if he will become sheriff and give them the town they want. After a lot of coaxing the young man agrees and sets out on the task of cleaning up the town.

The good town's people praise the young new sheriff for the many great deeds he does to give them the place they want to live in. They can now walk the streets without fear of their lives. However, the day comes for sacrifice. The powerful rancher's son comes to town, gets drunk and kills a man. The new sheriff arrests the drunk son and puts him in jail. The overbearing rancher finds out and sends word that he will kill the new sheriff and burn the town to the ground if his son is not released. The sheriff gathers the town's people, telling them "if we stick together now, you will have the town you want". The good town's people tell the sheriff they are behind him all the way. Shortly the great rancher rides into town with a hoard of men, giving the town twenty four hours to release his son. If they don't, he will carry out his threats to burn the town and make anyone that stands in his way pay with their lives.

The new sheriff once again gathered the town asking them for volunteers to ward off the rancher and his men. The good town's people responded with, "We don't want to be involved, we have families, that's why we hired you". He explained that the only way he could stand up for them is with their support. It was their town and they had to pay the price to have what they wanted. Their response, "Well, maybe we had better just give the rancher what he wants."

The moral I got from that show was that all those good people loved the life they had as long as they weren't the ones who had to stand up for it. No one in this country (the good town's people) gave a damn about this jerk in Vietnam. These people already had the life they wanted and they didn't have to stand up for it. I think this country looked at it as if this war mongering person strolled into another town and it was the other town's problem not theirs. We got what we want so screw everyone else.

The young man that became sheriff was no war monger or any super brave man. Just a man that knew nothing came easy and that if you believe in something you had to stand up for it. Also he was a man that believed in helping others achieve what they believed in. He was a good man with good beliefs. Why in the world would this guy sacrifice for these good town's people? Why in the world would the great young men that served in Vietnam sacrifice themselves for the good town's people of this country that had everything they wanted and could care less about anybody else? How could they sacrifice and have their homeland, all snug in their glorious freedoms that others died for, condemn them for what they did? Is there no one that understands this sheriff?

Suddenly the shock of the plane's tires striking the runway and the engines in reverse thrust yanked me back to reality. I sat up in my seat gathering my senses and looked to Alan.

"Well, we're here." He said.

"Yeah, I guess we are." I responded.

We quickly gathered our things and shuffled off the plane. After claiming our baggage we hailed a taxi and gave him the address of the Miami safe house. The taxi ride was accomplished in silence as was the long plane ride, each of us deep in our own thoughts. My thoughts continued with the young sheriff that stood up only to be down trodden by the very ones he sacrificed for.

All his deeds to tame the town, no matter how evil, were praised as long as they were kept distance from the good town's people. As long as his morels were the only ones sacrificed, as long as it didn't touch their lives or morels it was heroic. However, when it came upon the good town's people to be part of or condone his deeds, suddenly it was immoral and evil and the sheriff must be condemned for his actions.

Was it that now the acts of war that had given us the freedoms that we enjoy had become immoral, or was it that now, that we enjoyed that freedom, those acts to allow others those freedoms were immoral? Was it that acts of war were alright when they were committed to give us freedom but once we had those freedoms and others used those acts, the acts now became evil and immoral.

The words from the taxi driver, "Twenty seven sixty", once again interrupted my minds wondering through the analogy of the country to the sheriff.

"Thanks." Alan responded as we each handed him a twenty dollar bill.

"Hey, thanks guys. You want some help with those bags?"

"Nah, we can handle it." I said as I grabbed my bags.

Once inside the safe house, Alan and I sat our bags down by the front door and headed for the bar. As we fixed a scotch and water, A.J. laid down his pool cue and came toward us with his hand extended. "Hey guys, how ya doing?"

"Alright, I guess. How about you?" I answered as I grasped his hand.

Shrugging his shoulders, A.J. answered, "Alright."

"Anything happening?" Alan asked.

"Not yet. I guess there's a lot of shit going on in the Middle East though." A.J. retorted. "The colonel said to stand by and he'd have a briefing tomorrow or the next day."

"What kind of shit?" I inquired.

"I'm not sure. My guess is that the Shah is having trouble with the war with Iraq."

"You think they might have us go in?" Alan asked as he handed me my drink.

"I don't know. You guys know Thompson's team, don't you?"

Alan and I both nodded as we took a long gulp of our scotch and responded by saying, "You've told us some stories about them, but we haven't met them personally."

"Well anyway, they're on their way over there somewhere now, but no one knows where or why, or at least no one is saying." A.J. said as he reached into his pocket and pulled out his vile of cocaine and held it out to us.

"Thanks, I need some of that." I said as I accepted the vile.

"What the hell could they have us doing over there?" Alan inquired.

A.J. shrugged his shoulders as he walked around behind the bar to fix himself a drink.

I reached over to the end of the bar and grabbed a little tray and poured two large lines of cocaine out from the vile. After picking up the straw that was lying by the tray, I sucked down one of the lines with one large inhaling action then handed the tray and straw to Alan and asked, "Anything been said about us going back to Nam and getting those guys out?"

"Not really." A.J. responded as he accepted his vile back from me and poured himself out a line on the tray that Alan had just handed him. "Someone said that we were going to try to handle it diplomatically."

"Yeah right!" I blurted out.

We stayed up all night drinking, snorting cocaine and discussing the problems of the world. None of us had any answers but we had lots of problems.

The sun was already up when the colonel entered the room. "Jesus Christ, you guys look like shit." He said.

"I don't feel bad at all, yet." I retorted.

He chuckled and said, "A.J. get your team together and get ready to leave within forty eight hours."

"Roger, roger, sir." A.J. responded as he stood up. "But where we going?"

"I'll give you all that when I brief you just before you leave. Prepare for an extended mission though. Have the entire team here by eighteen hundred hours tonight and no one leaves the house from that time on. The team is on standby."

"Everyone's here now sir, except Willie and Ray. Willie is right here in Miami, he won't be a problem. But Ray went out to California. I don't know if he can get back here that quick." Explained A.J.

"See what you can do, we're going to need him. Tell him to get the first flight back and be here ASAP."

"Right on, sir."

"Well, I'm going to go get me a shower and a good meal before we get locked in this place." I said as I stood up.

"Me too." Echoed Alan.

"You guys wait till I make the calls to Willie and Ray, and I'll join you. I have a feeling it might be the last time we get some good old American cooking for a while." Responded A.J.

Colonel Myers gave us a half smirky grin and a semi salute as he grabbed his briefcase and headed for his office. "See you boys soon."

CHAPTER 40

"Fifteen two, fifteen four, fifteen six, fifteen eight, and a double run of eight makes sixteen." I announced as I moved my peg along the cribbage board.

"I only got two, four, six, and a pair for eight." Alan responded. "What did you give me in the crib?"

"Nothing, I hope."

"Well almost nothing, a run of three."

A knock on our door came just as I picked up the cards and began to shuffle them. "Come on in." I yelled.

The door opened and A.J. stuck his head in, "Hey guys, the colonel is here and he's going to brief us now. So come on down."

"Right now?" I asked pointing to the cribbage board, "I got a skunk going here."

"Yeah, right now."

"A.J. you got great timing, thanks." Alan said as he stood up laughing. "He's never been able to skunk me yet."

"Yeah, well we're going to pick this game up right where we left off right after the briefing." I stated, starting for the door.

"I doubt that I'll have time then, we'll probably be awfully busy."

"Bull shit!" I retorted as we reached the bottom of the stairs.

Alan was still laughing when we entered the briefing room and sat down. Frank and Charlie came in right behind us and shut the door.

"Everyone's here colonel, except Ray," A.J. announced, "and he's due in at sixteen twenty this afternoon."

"Alright, that will work out ok. Now guys, at nineteen hundred hours today the van will be here to take you to the airport. I want everyone ready to leave by that time. Store all your personnel things here, everything you need will be given to you when you reach your destination." Colonel Myers face was serious as he spoke.

"Colonel, what might our destination be?" Don asked.

"As of right now all I can tell you is that you are going to the Middle East."

"Sir, what the hell we going to do over there?" Bobby inquired.

"I can't tell you that yet. You'll be met at your destination and taken to a compound. I'll be there within forty eight hours of your arrival and hopefully be able to give you more details then. Right now everything is very hush hush." By the look in the colonel's eye and the way he spoke, I, along with everyone else, knew he didn't know much more about this mission. However, we also knew that by his demeanor, he was worried about something on this one.

A little after five that afternoon Ray arrived at the safe house, "Alright guys, what the hell is so important that I had to hurry back here to all your ugly faces."

"We couldn't stand you out there having all the fun without us." Alan blurted out.

"Go to hell! No really, what's up?"

"You got about an hour and a half to store your gear." A.J. explained. "We leave here at nineteen hundred for the middle east."

"What the hell are we going to do over there?" Ray asked.

"We don't know yet. We won't find out till we're there." A.J. came back.

"A.J. the colonel said that everything we need we'll get when we get there." Willie directed his comment to A.J. as he was heading for the bar.

"Yeah, what about it?"

"Well, as I hear it, those damn Arabs over there are against booze. The only way you can buy anything is on the black market, and if you get caught they put your ass away."

"Willie, when have you ever worried about the law or jail?" I said bringing a laugh from everyone. "However, A.J., he's got a good point. Someone had better make sure I got a couple of bottles of good scotch when we get there."

"Sometimes I wonder about you guys." A.J. rebutted. "You know we've never had any problem getting booze or anything else for that matter, and I don't think we'll have any trouble this time either."

"Well just in case, I think I better have a couple of stiff ones before we go. Just in case you understand." I commented on my way to the bar.

"John, you've never needed an excuse to drink before, why start now?" Don cried out.

"Screw You!" I blurted out.

"Alright you guys." A.J. intervened, "Let's get our shit ready, you know the colonel said be ready by nineteen hundred and you know that's what he means."

CHAPTER 41

After twenty two hours in the air and a short layover at Heathrow, we finally landed in Ishfahan, Iran. It was late afternoon and a dry hot breeze blew across the airport like someone was trying to dry the dessert with a giant hair dryer. You could see the ripples of the heat rising from the tarmac runway, creating a dreamy image.

The plane was immediately met by several armed guards, quickly separating us from the rest of the passengers. While the other passengers were shuffled off to customs, we were escorted to a near by hanger where a small buss awaited.

"Alright guys, our limousine awaits," A.J. mocked pointing at the bus, "It will sweep us off to our awaiting castle."

"I sure as hell hope its got air conditioning!" Skip quipped.

"It has." One of the awaiting officials said as he swung his arm toward the door, "Please," motioning for us to board.

"Certainly James." Alan eloquently stated as he boarded the bus.

The bus ride took us about twenty minutes through the outskirts of town. We finally pulled up to the gates of an isolated compound surrounded by a ten foot concrete wall. One of the two armed guards at the gate came to the door of the bus. Our escorting official opened the door and spoke to him in a language that sounded more like a drunken slur than audible words. The guard immediately returned to the other guard and they quickly opened the gate, allowing the bus to pass.

As the bus pulled through the gate toward the largest of three buildings on the compound, I was in awe. We had expected to be taken to some drab place to plan whatever mission we were assigned, instead we were taken to what might be classified as a small palace.

The outside of the buildings were inlaid with small blue and white tiles creating a beautiful mosque.

Stopping in front of the largest of the three buildings which looked more like an elegant office complex than a house, our escort motioned for us to exit the bus and said, "Gentlemen, Please."

We exited the bus and were taken on a tour of the castle. Upstairs there were a dozen bedrooms complete with all the amenities. Also, four complete bathrooms all done in masterfully arranged colored tiles. Downstairs we were led through a giant kitchen, which any woman would have died for but we couldn't have cared less about, and three living areas. Still in awe of the house we were about to inhabit, our guide led us to the back patio where there was an almost Olympic size swimming pool. The entire patio area was, once again, done in colorful tile patterns and had numerous lounging chairs and an umbrella patio table.

Once our tour was completed we went back to the front of the house where our escort informed us that the second building closest to the main house was set up for whatever we chose. It had several large rooms and was sound proof. The other building was for the guards and servants.

"These three men," Our escort began, pointing to the three men that met us at the door, "will serve your needs here. There will be two guards at the gate at all times and two guards walking the grounds. If you should require anything please see Sergeant Reizies here. Now if there is nothing further I can do for you right now, I must leave."

"I think we'll be just fine sir." A.J. said with a smile and a slight bow of his head.

"The only thing that's missing is a harem." Charlie interjected.

"I am sorry, I can do nothing about that for you. However, Sergeant Reizies here might be able to arrange something to satisfy your needs. Oh yes, your Colonel Myers has said that you are not to leave the compound."

"We already figured that." A.J. answered.

"Fine. I must go now." Our escort stated as he rejoined the awaiting bus driver.

The night air was dry and still as I laid in one of the lounging chairs by the pool looking up at the stars that were starting to break through the darkening sky. Alan, Doug, Charlie and Skip were at the pool side table playing poker as Ray and Willie sat back and heckled them. Larry was inside reading one of the books he had found called, Crash Of 79, which was about what was going to happen here in the Middle East. The colonel had arrived about an hour earlier and he and A.J. were out in the house that we were going to use as our operations building. The colonel had set a zero eight hundred hours briefing in the morning and he and A.J. were planning that briefing.

I took a long pull from my scotch, thinking that maybe Sergeant Reizes really could get almost anything we wanted. As I looked up at the stars winking back at me, my mind began to wonder, what the hell were we going to do here. This war between Iran and Iraq had been going on for a very long time and of course we openly backed the Shah. The Shah was one of the largest buyers of American arms and technology in the world, but that wasn't the only reason that we supported him. The United States needed Arab oil, and the Arab world was in great turmoil right now.

The Arab world had no significance to us or the rest of the world until the discovery of oil here. Although the majority of the Arab people were still poor, heads of the Arab countries had amassed great fortunes from the production of their oil. Almost every major oil company in the world had an office in the Middle East and their views were as varied as the countries themselves. With the wealth that the heads of these countries now had, they found themselves thrust to the forefront of world politics. The Arabs had been shunned by the world. They had been considered third world countries and now found themselves being wined and dined by all the world heads of state who once had shunned them. The new found wealth and the change in the acceptance of the Arab world came so fast that it created a turmoil among the heads of the Arab countries as well as a turmoil with the rest of the world. Each country's leader loved the power that their new wealth had brought them and contrived against their brother to feed their thirst of power and wealth.

The United States needed to have a stabling force in the Middle East, not only for its need of their oil but as a major world power. The U.S. worked, aided and did all the diplomatic things with the Prince of Saudi Arabia and all the other nations to make sure we maintained our influence in the Arab world. However, the Shah was thought to be our biggest hook into the Middle East. If we could keep him as our puppet we would be ensured our hand hold on one of the most powerful groups in the world. What was in the Shah's best interest was actually what was in our best interest, and whatever it took to keep him in the fore front of the Arab world became paramount to us. It was thought that the stabilization of the United States depended a lot on the stabilization of the Arab world. I personally didn't think that was true, but who the hell was I.

"Hey guys." A.J. interrupted my thoughts as he came onto the patio.

"You get all our strategies worked out?" I responded getting up to go and fix myself another drink.

"Well I think you're going to find out tomorrow at the briefing." A.J. answered.

"A.J. get your money out and get over here in this game." Doug bellowed. "I need some sucker that I can beat, Alan here is whipping my ass bad."

"Ohhh no! I'm going to bed and get a good nights sleep for a change, and I suggest you guys do the same."

"What the hell you trying to do, get a promotion?" Willie sneered.

"Screw you Willie! Hey why the hell is everyone on my ass anyway?"

"We're not A.J. it's just that we love you." Alan stated. "Com'on Charlie, it's your bet."

"Yeah right. Well I'll see you all in the morning." A.J. said as he headed in the house.

"I guess I'll turn in too." I announced. "Good night ya all."

CHAPTER 42

The early morning breeze was still cool as it gently rippled through the patio area where I was having my morning coffee. I awoke early and had come down to the pool to enjoy the dawning sun. "How beautiful the breaking of daylight is." I thought to myself. The silence of the sun beginning to climb the sky was broken when Alan emerged onto the patio.

"What's up?" He said sipping his coffee.

"Not much." I answered shrugging my shoulders. "Just the sun I guess."

"Yeah, it sure looks like it's getting there." He responded.

"You win or lose last night?" I asked.

"Oh, I won a couple hundred I guess."

The patio began to come alive now as each of the team began to file out clutching their coffee cups. Not much was said as each of us tried to absorb energy from the sun and coffee like charging our battery.

Colonel Myers stepped out. Stretching his arms out and yawning, he said, "Great morning, huh boys?"

"Yeah." Came the answer almost in unison.

"Well let me grab a cup of coffee and you boys refill your cups and let's get this briefing started. Ok?" He said as he turned and began to walk inside.

We all stood up and followed the colonel through the kitchen and out the front door like a gaggle of geese. "There will be an armed guard at this door twenty four hours a day now." He said nodding toward the soldier by the door he was opening. "Now these two rooms." He was pointing to his left, "will be our planning rooms, and that one back there is my office, off limits of course. And this one," pointing to his right, "will be our briefing room. Go on in and take a seat."

The room had a very large conference table in it with chairs along one side and both ends. On the other side there was only one chair, we all knew that belonged to the colonel. We rambled in and took seats around the table. The colonel came in behind us, shut the door and took the lone side chair.

"Alright," He began, "to start with, nothing, as in all our missions, nothing from now on leaves this building. Anything said or done in here stays in here. Again, nothing, no matter how trivial, will be talked about outside of here, not even in the main quarters. I have made sure that this is secure in here and I mean nothing leaves here. Is that clear?"

"Yes sir." We all responded.

"Now, I guess the next thing I'll tell you is what we're here for." The colonel began to explain why it was important that we help the Shah. He went through the propaganda of the importance of the Shah and the importance of our role. "The United States' role here," He continued, "in this war against Iraq, is one of an advisory role. We all know that means that we can't get caught actually participating in it, and we all know what that means." The colonel stopped and looked over to A.J. "How about telling that guard out there to send for a couple of pots of coffee, I'm almost empty."

A.J. stood up, went to the door and told the guard to send for coffee. For the next ten minutes, until the coffee got there, the colonel went on about the deniablity of our actions should we get caught or anything at all went wrong. After we had all refilled our cups the colonel got to the meat of our briefing, our mission.

"Alright gentlemen, here's what you're here for. You have been sent here for one of the biggest and toughest jobs of your life. I know it's one of my biggest." He paused, pressed his lips together and looked everyone in the eye before continuing. "You're job is to kill Sadam Hussaine."

A hush fell over the room being broken by Doug's, "NO SHIT?"

"No Shit," Answered the colonel with a slight nod and a forced pressed lip half grin.

"That's a pretty tall order, isn't it sir?" Skip queried.

"Yeah, it is." Colonel Myers responded, "But it's been deemed necessary and possible. Now it's our job to figure out how and get it done."

A.J. jumped in, "The colonel and I, last night, started looking over all the intelligence reports we have and there's a lot. Starting today each of us is going to take a bundle, carefully go through it and find a chink in Hussaine's armor."

"Do we have any idea what kind of chink we're looking for?" Alan asked.

"Not really." Colonel Myers responded. "The Iranians have tried almost everything. They've tried all kinds of assassination attempts, bombings and heaven knows what else."

"Sir," I began. "I think I'm a little confused here. What makes anyone think that we can get to this jerk? The Iranians, who can sneak in and around Iraq much easier than we can, couldn't get close enough to get it done?"

"Well, that's a good question. I guess because they haven't been successful maybe they think that an outside source will have an idea that will work. At any rate we've been given the task so let's not waste time on why we were given this assignment, but on how we accomplish it. Ok?"

"I'm sorry sir, I didn't mean to bitch about why," I began to retort, but was interrupted by Colonel Myers.

"I know John, but this one's going to be stressful for all of us. The company is really watching us and trying to put their ideas in about what to do and everything else. We just need to get it done."

"Yes sir." I answered.

"Alright, A.J. why don't you get what we have so far and let's get started. If we find something and need anything special, it's no problem. We have Carte Blanche on this one. Any questions?" After a pause and no response from us the colonel continued, "Ok then, lets get started. I've got another meeting but I'll be back this afternoon. Well, A.J. take over."

A.J. handed us each a stack of intelligence reports, "Now what I want you to do is read over everything you've got there and make notes on anything, and I mean anything, that you think might be useful. However I don't want to stop and discuss every little thing. Lets all get through what we have, then we'll go through our notes and brainstorm. Ok?" A.J. received just a nod from us as we began to read the reports.

The only sounds in the room were the scratching of pens on paper, as each man carefully began to analyze the material he had. We steadfastly worked through lunch and on into the late afternoon, scrutinizing every word in the reports. Finally the silence of tense concentration was broken by A.J. "Alright guys, let's take a break for the day, before we pop a seam in our brains."

"I'm for that," Skip commented, "This son of a bitch is some kind of security freak."

"That must be why he's still alive." I stated.

"Yeah!" A.J. said. "Let's knock off now and go on up to the house. The colonel should be back any time and hopefully he'll have some more for us to look at tomorrow."

"Oh great, more reading." Alan said. "Right now I need a drink."

For the next three days we grappled with every little flaw this man had. The same problem kept coming up. He very seldom put himself in a position of vulnerability. When he was vulnerable, like out in public, he was so well covered that an attempt on his life would be suicide.

After sifting through endless dead ends Alan hit on something, "You know, there's one thing this guy doesn't like to do."

"What's that?" I asked.

"Fly." Alan continued, "Whenever he travels, it's always by car. Isn't it?"

"Yeah, I seen that too." A.J. responded half heartedly. "But, he travels in a caravan of bullet proof vehicles accompanied by a company of armed guards. Also, you never know which car he's in."

Willie interjected, "And he never makes his travel plans known, or where he even is for that matter."

"I know all that, but just listen for a minute." Alan pleaded. "First, armored vehicles aren't a problem. We can always use armor piercing or ARPs, a lot of things. The problem is only getting the right intelligence."

"Only!" A.J. rebutted. "Only, is the big thing that makes it unworkable."

"No A.J., I'm not so sure about that." Alan began to explain. "If, and I realize it's a big if, but if we can pinpoint his location at any certain time we would have a shot at it."

"I think I'm starting to follow you Alan." I interjected. "If we have an exact location we have a starting point."

"That's right." Alan took back over. "Once we have that fact we know he has to leave there sometime for somewhere else. Now, if we can get one of those Iranian moles close enough to give us a few hours notice of his travel, we might have a shot at him."

Doug spoke up, "Alan you're God dam crazy! There's no way we can scout a route, get there, prepare and make a hit with only a few hours notice."

"No wait a minute here guys," A.J. came back with a grin coming onto his face as if a light just went on in his head. "You might have something here. We know, from his past movement, that he really only stays in four or five locations, and we know what those are."

"Exactly!" Alan responded.

"What we could do is plan for all the different routes from all those points. Then when we know where he's going we correspond to the precise plan for that route." A.J. was starting to like the plan.

"All that sounds good, but we'll need more than a few hours to get there and set up." Charlie commented.

"Not necessarily." I jumped in. "We can have preselected staging areas for each location, once we know his location we head for that staging area. He usually stays at one place a couple of days. That gives us time to get to the staging area and be ready for the news of his route, then head for that plan."

"Yeah, I think we got the start of something here. Let's see what the colonel thinks." A.J. said as he stood and headed for the colonel's office.

A.J. quickly returned with Colonel Myers and we began to explain the basic idea. It was a rough idea but the colonel knew we would refine it to split second timing.

"Well, there are some holes, but I'm sure you can close them." The colonel said. "However the whole thing depends on the intelligence we can get. Let me make some calls and see what we can get. I'll let you guys know in the morning."

The morning air was already like a hot breath blowing gently on us as we headed for our meeting with Colonel Myers. Once inside, everyone took their seats at the conference table where the colonel was already seated.

"Good morning men," he began. "Lets get right down to it. I don't know if we got anything here or not. First let me tell you what I found out then we'll see what you got to say. The best intelligence we can get and the most accurate, is that they can give us his exact location only after he's actually there. Then as for when and where he is going, the best we can do is when he leaves the source can tell us what road he is taking out of town and that he is leaving now."

"Jesus! That sure cuts the hell out of our time. That's the best they can do?" I inquired.

"Yep, that's the best."

"Back to the books." Skip exasperatedly said.

"Well now wait just a minute here." A.J. announced. "All that means is that we'll have real accurate intelligence reports, something we don't always get."

"That's no shit." Doug agreed.

"It also means that our time table will be extremely tight," Alan announced, "but not impossible."

"I agree. In fact it may be to our advantage, because of their tight security of times and destinations, they won't expect a planned hit." I added.

"That's right." A.J. was directing his comments to Colonel Myers. "Let us have a couple of days to see what we can work up on this, sir. I think we might have a chance here. Don't you guys think so?" He added looking around at us.

Colonel Myers looked around the room as we all shrugged and nodded agreement, then he spoke, "Alright, but we need to come up with something quick, cause I'm getting pressure."

The planning began immediately. We went back through the reports and studied maps and charts, and piece by piece, a plan began to take shape. Two days later we called the colonel in to brief him on what we came up with.

A.J. began explaining the entire plan to the colonel while the rest of us sat watching for expressions on the face of Colonel Myers. At the end of the briefing A.J. handed him a list saying, "We've got a little work left to do on timing, but we should have it down by the time you get this list of armament and supplies we'll need."

Pressing his lips together and slightly nodding his head while still looking down at the map, Colonel Myers responded, "Looks and sounds good, but do you really think it will work?"

"It's the best we got sir." A.J. stated as we all agreed.

"Alright, I'll get started on this list right now, you guys get those fine points worked out."

CHAPTER 43

It took the colonel two days to acquire all the armament, equipment and supplies needed for our assassination plot. He arranged for everything to be delivered to a little abandoned airfield, about ten miles from our compound, and the Iranians provided security with a company of armed soldiers.

During these two days we ironed out every minute detail of our plot. There were four basic plans, one for each known location. Each plan had two to three contingency plans for the probable routes that would be taken by Sadahm. The known locations each had a point alpha. Once we knew of Sadahm's presence at one of our known locations, we would select the corresponding plan and proceed to that point alpha. Upon arriving at point alpha, we would wait for word of his departure and then select the corresponding contingency plan for that route. All this looked great on paper, however we knew that when the word came and the contingency plan selected, it would take split second timing to accomplish the assassination of Sadahm Hussaine.

After all the gear was delivered to the airfield, we spent a whole day arranging it. The portions that would be needed for all four plans were loaded onto the helicopter, the rest was separated into four groups corresponding to the plan it was needed for. Everything possible was done to minimize our loading and departure time once we got the order.

Now came the hard part. The wait. We were now on total standby alert. The word of Sadahm's location could come at any moment and we had to be ready.

The late afternoon sun had begun to fade and the day's heat started to leave the desert on the fourth day of our wait when A.J.'s voice rang throughout the house, "Alright guys! We got a mission!"

Everyone scrambled from wherever they happened to be and in a matter of seconds the bus driver was pulling away from the compound and speeding for the airfield. Within minutes we would be at the airfield and soon after that on our way.

"Now we're going with plan charlie, here John, these are the charts and maps you'll need for charlie. The colonel is already on his way to the airfield and will have winds and weather for you when we get there." A.J. said.

"It won't take long to calculate things." I responded accepting the charts and maps. "What about refueling? Did he get it cleared?"

"I'm sure he did, but we'll ask him before we go. Ok?"

The bus driver barely slowed as the armed guard waved us through the gate. We screeched to a halt in front of the hanger and scurried off the bus. Each man went about his assigned tasks preparing for our departure and soon the hum of a busy bee hive filled the hanger. I spotted the colonel in the back of the hanger and quickly made my way toward him.

As I neared, he spoke, "John you're going to have scattered overcast at two thousand and winds are two eight zero at eight to ten."

"Roger." I responded as I walked past him to a desk against the back wall. Unfolding the maps A.J. had given me, I began the last minute flight calculations. It only took a couple of minutes of figuring and I was just finishing as the rest of the team was pushing the helicopter outside.

"John, you ready yet?" A.J. called to me.

"On my way." I answered as I began to walk toward the helicopter, now outside.

When I reached the aircraft, everyone was aboard except A.J. He was standing by my door with Colonel Myers. I opened my door and spoke to them as I reached in, handing my maps and charts to Alan sitting in the copilots seat. "I got it at about two thirty to Bakhtaran and thirty minutes there to refuel. We are cleared there for refueling, aren't we sir?"

"Right." He answered.

"Then one forty five to point alpha. That's about a four and a half hour arrival time." I finished.

"Right. Lets hit it." A.J. said climbing aboard.

"Roger that." I responded buckling my seatbelt.

"God's speed, boys." The colonel said as he backed away from the aircraft giving us his standard half salute.

Sadahm was at a town called Al Mawsil, which was about two hundred and fifty miles to the north of Baghdad. We had selected a spot about fifty miles to the east of Al Mawsil as point alpha. Point alpha was out in the desert to the west of the mountains but still offered us some good cover. We needed good cover because we did not know how long we would have to wait for Sadahm's departure. The wait was a big risk because the longer the wait the more chance there was of being discovered.

It was a calm night with no turbulence as the aircraft cut through the darkness like a knife. The first leg of our flight to Bakhtaran took exactly two hours and thirty minutes. As I set the helicopter down I said, "Damn I'm good A.J., two thirty on the nose."

"Yeah, well just see to it that the rest of the timing on this job comes out that close." He responded.

"Shit A.J. where's your sense of adventure?" Alan quipped.

"Back in Miami." A.J. laughed. "Come on, lets get this son a bitch refueled and in the air."

"Roger." I said as I opened my door and got out.

It took only about twenty minutes for the Iranians to top off the fuel tank. Once they finished I checked the fuel cap to make sure it was secure then again took my place in the pilot's seat.

"The easy part's over now," I said as the engine wined, building up RPM, "with this overcast its going to be pretty dark and flying low level, I'll need all the eyes we got."

"No problem," A.J. answered, "we'll all be watching back here."

"The boarder's probably going to have troops all over it." Alan interjected.

"Yeah, well let's hope they don't make us." I said as we lifted off.

The light film of clouds precluded any natural light. It was so dark that we all had to strain to make out the silhouettes of major landmarks to pinpoint our location. I knew my biggest problem was yet to come however. The landing at point alpha.

"We should be coming up on the boarder anytime now." Alan announced.

"Ok, I'm going to add about ten minutes, maybe twenty, to our flight A.J." I stated.

"Why? What's wrong?" He asked.

"Nothing's wrong, but I think it would be a good idea if we turn to the west southwest to cross." I was already turning. "This way if any Iraqi troops make us, they'll think were headed for Baghdad."

"Good idea," Came A.J.'s response. "But why did you just now think of it?"

"Shit! You're lucky I thought of it at all." I answered.

After we were sure we had crossed the boarder I turned back to the north. I was trying to keep the mountains off to my right side and also make sure I passed to the east of Kirkuk. The city of Kirkuk was a major landmark for me, as it would mean I was nearing point alpha, however I didn't want to be to close to it. It was now nearing eleven thirty at night and being spotted flying around that time of night would surely arouse suspicion.

"Ok John, I think alpha should be about right over there at our ten o'clock." Alan said.

"Yeah, right about that clump of trees there, ya think?" I responded.

"Yeah."

"A.J." I called.

"Yeah, what's up?"

"How bout opening the doors back there and keep me clear. I'm coming in a little hot."

"You got it."

As soon as the skids touched the ground everyone scampered off the aircraft. I quickly began shutting down the engine while the others scouted the area. When the rotors came to a stop, the helicopter was tied down and concealed from sight.

"Let's dig in and get some rest now." A.J. was saying. "Doug you got the first watch and you all know the order after that. Remember, and I repeat, remember, whoever's on watch, you listen to every little bit of static on the radio. They're going to broadcast our go signal only once. Everyone got that?"

"We know." We acknowledged.

Doug was the one who was to stay awake first on watch, however none of us could sleep. We all sat around the radio in the cool night air, snorting cocaine and waiting for the darkness to disappear.

We had landed around midnight. Now the sun was beginning to climb the horizon. Suddenly the silence was broken by the radio, "Wolf Pack, King Cobra, Number One." Then silence again. Wolf pack, that was us, king cobra, that was Sadahm Hussaine, and number one, that was his route.

Skip, Doug, Alan and I immediately sprang to our feet and began disrobing the helicopter of its camouflage net. The rest gathered the radio and other equipment removed from the aircraft and replaced it there. A.J. quickly opened the map and spread it out on the ground where we all gathered around for a last minute briefing.

"God Damn it!" A.J. cursed. "He's going south. I hoped he'd go north."

"Oh, what the hell." I said. "Look at it this way, it makes our exit shorter."

"Yeah, well here's the route guys." A.J.'s finger was tracing it on the map. "Are there any last minute questions?" After a short silence he continued, "Ok then, let's get this shit over with."

We had picked an attack point about seventy miles south of Al Mowsil. The highway was to the west of us and the Figrish River to our east. There was a large hill where we made our base point. From this hill we would launch the rockets. Doug, Skip and Larry were set up here with RPG rocket launchers along with A.J., Ray and myself to load for them. Alan, Charlie and Willie were down below with M16 rifles and hand grenades. They would do the final clean up sweep.

Both A.J. and I kept our binoculars trained on the road watching for the caravan caring Sadahm. "There they come." A.J. announced.

"Yeah, but something's wrong A.J." I said. "Where the hell is the escort troops? I only see the three limos."

"Damn. Where the hell could they be?"

"I don't know. What do you want to do?" I asked. "They could just be laying back, which is going to really mess up our timing."

167

"Yeah, I know, but we ain't got time to make any changes and we're here now." A.J. said as he handed the binoculars to Ray, then continued, "Ok, Doug you got limo number one, Skip number two and Larry you got three. After your first shot make sure you got a hit then we'll reload you, fire your second shot we'll reload you again and then watch for a troop carrier that might be coming late. If it comes, all three of you hit it. Got it?"

After he got an acknowledgment from us A.J. let out a loud whistle, signaling the other three below. They answered with two return whistles.

Doug, Skip and Larry were lying prone on the ground, aiming the launchers at the road below, as A.J., Ray and myself knelt beside them. We had them loaded, ready to fire and the next round in our hands.

"Hold on now, wait till they get just past that bend," A.J. continued to talk, "I'll tell you when, hold on, hold on, hold onnnnn-OK FIRE!"

Doug fired first then Skip then Larry. Each round hit its target, the engine area of each limo. The vehicles came to an abrupt stop with smoke bellowing from the front end. We had the three shooters reloaded and tapped them on the head to let them know. Whoosh, Whoosh, Whoosh. The second rounds found there way through the bullet proof glass and exploded inside of each vehicle.

We reloaded the shooters once again, then I began surveying the highway. Alan, Charlie and Willie began running for the limos. They sprayed the inside of the vehicles with their M16s then started tossing debris around the area to make it look like a rebel attack.

"I don't see anything coming, A.J." I announced.

"Alright let's head for the bird. Com'on guys lets get the hell out of here."

Each of us grabbed the gear we were assigned to carry and rumbled down the hill. When we reached the aircraft I threw the gear I was carrying into the back, then climbed in the pilot's seat and started the engine. By the time the other three arrived I had full RPM and once they were aboard I pulled pitch. We were off, heading for the Iranian boarder.

"A.J. there's something wrong with this hit." Alan said.

"I know. It sure don't feel right." I responded.

"No." A.J. commanded. "There wasn't anyone alive, was there?"

"No. Shit the RPGs gutted everything before we ever got there." Alan answered.

As I pulled the aircraft to a hover back at the airfield, I could see the colonel standing in front of the hanger beside the bus. I searched his face for a clue to what his mood was, but as usual, his stone face gave me nothing. I gently set the helicopter on the ground and he began to walk towards us as I rolled the throttle back and shut down the engine.

With a half salute he began to speak as we began to disembark the aircraft. "Boys, lets get the bird in the hanger then board the bus. We'll debrief back at the compound."

"Roger." Came the response to him.

The ground handling wheels were put on the helicopter then quickly rolled into the hanger. We then filed onto the bus and made the trip back to the compound without a word spoken. Upon arrival at the compound we strolled straight to the briefing house and took a seat.

"Any news yet colonel?" A.J. asked for the first time.

"No not yet. There was something about a rebel attack but nothing said about Sadahm." He responded.

"Something's wrong here." Alan interjected.

"Maybe they're just trying to hide the fact." Doug stated.

"I don't know." The colonel came back shaking his head. "Something like that is pretty hard to keep quiet. Well, you boys go on up to the house and A.J. you stay and brief me."

The rest of us headed straight for the bar upon entering the house. After taking a big gulp of my scotch, I grabbed the small tray on the bar and laid out a large line of cocaine. Feeling the immediate rush to my head from snorting the white powder, I quickly killed my drink and fixed another. Half way through my second drink one of the guards entered the room announcing that the colonel wanted us.

"Well boys," The colonel began, "we just got word. The mission was a bust."

"Damn! What the hell happened?" I exclaimed.

"You hit Sadahm's caravan alright, however he wasn't in it." The colonel explained. "It looks like he decided at the last minute to fly to

Baghdad rather than drive. They're keeping it quiet cause they think it's local rebels."

"Where in the hell do we get our intelligence from anyway?" Alan asked. "We risked our asses to wipe out three of his God dam cars that he probably has already replaced."

"Calm down." A.J. spoke up. "There's nothing we can do about it now."

"Yeah but - "Alan began but was interrupted by A.J.

"Yeah but nothing. It's all over, let's just get on with whatever's next."

CHAPTER 44

The next three days were spent drinking, snorting cocaine and lounging by the pool. Soon, everyone hoped, we would get some word as to what was next, and soon it was.

"Hey guys." A.J. announced as he stepped on to the patio, "We got a oh nine hundred briefing tomorrow."

At zero nine hundred, we all set around the briefing table, drinking our morning coffee and waiting for the colonel to appear from his office. The tensions, that had been building over the last three days, were already fading. We knew there was another job and there would be no more time for brooding over our last failed mission.

The colonel came in the room, shut the door and headed straight for his chair. Without any hesitation he unfolded a large tactical map and displayed it in front of us. "Ok men, this mission will be in conjunction with the Iranians. In other words an Iranian team is going with you. Now as you can see, Baghdad is almost due west of us, and right here," Pointing to a spot, a little northwest of Baghdad along the Euphrates River, "is what we believe to be a plant that makes the poison gas that Sadahm is using against the Iranians. The Iranians have made a bunch of bombing runs on it but can't seem to knock it out. You guys are going to take it out. By eleven hundred tomorrow we'll have the air photos of it and charts of what we think the lay out is. We have the basic plan already but you have until Friday, that gives you three days, to refine it. On Friday we will meet with the Iranian leaders of the squad you're taking in, and brief them. Mission launch is Monday morning."

"Sir," Alan started, "That place has got to be heavily guarded. What about troop intelligence reports? Can we even get close to it on the ground?"

171

"All the intelligence reports," A.J. jumped in, "Are in the planning room. We also have all the tactical and flight maps we need."

"You will also receive updated reports daily," The colonel added.

"For the rest of the day," A.J. continued, "I want all of you to read all the reports we have and study the maps to get an idea of the overlay. Then we'll all be back tomorrow at eleven hundred to look at the photos and charts then start refining this."

"Does anyone have anything else?" The colonel asked.

We all shook our heads no as we stood up.

"Fine, I've got another meeting to go to this afternoon, so I'll leave you to your work and see you tonight." The colonel said as he was leaving the room. He always had a meeting to go to.

We went across the hall to one of the planning rooms where A.J. took reports from the safe and handed one to each of us. "Each of you study each one of these until you know what all of them say. I'll be next door working on the map, when you're done here come over there. Ok?" A.J. received just a nod from us as we began to read the intelligence reports.

The reports were in depth but still sketchy without the photos and charts. It appeared that this plant was a fortress with, depending what the photos and charts showed, one major flaw. Of course a lot more study was needed, but the chink in their armor might just be the river side of the plant.

After about three and a half hours of going through the reports we went next door to where the maps and A.J. were. A.J. began showing us on a detailed map the path of the river and how right at the bend of the river it looked like some of the water was siphoned off and ran through the plant.

"You know A.J., we won't know till we see those other photos and charts, but that spot right there might just be the crack we need." I commented.

"Yeah, but from what I see," Ray interjected, "there's going to be a lot of ifs in this plan."

"There's always a lot of ifs in our plans Ray." Alan said.

"Well it's our job to limit those ifs." A.J. stated. "Now if no one has anything else, lets go up to the house and eat and relax for the night."

"What do those photos show?" I asked as Alan and I entered the planning room the next day.

"We just started looking at them." A.J. answered. "Here you guys start looking through these."

I accepted the stack of photos that A.J. held out to me and handed half to Alan as I asked, "What about the charts showing the insides?"

"Ray and Skip have those next door." Replied A.J.

There were about two hundred aerial photos for us to go through. Most were of little help, but we managed to pick out about eight or ten that actually depicted the different parts of the plant.

"It sure looks like they got it fortified real good from air strikes." Doug commented.

"Yeah," Alan answered. "They probably feel that's the real threat. Ya know though, they probably only have enough security to hold off small rebel attacks. Ya think?"

"I don't know." Charlie came back as he pointed to one of the photos. "Look here, this is most likely the main part of the plant, and this looks like the troop quarters area. It looks like it's big enough to hold quite a few men."

"Look at this guys." Larry interrupted.

"What about it?" I asked. "It just looks like the area to the east of the plant to me."

"It is." Larry continued, "But look at these railroad tracks here."

"Well that's probably how they ship in supplies and ship the gas to Baghdad." Alan added.

"It's not going to do any good to take out the tracks." Willie said. "They'd have them back up in no time."

"You aren't thinking that we could gain entry using the train cars, are you?" Alan asked. "Because it looks like here where the tracks cross the river to the plant there's a guard post."

"That's what I'm saying." Larry went on, "and here just north of the bridge, looks like more troop quarters."

"I don't remember reading anything yesterday about troops around the plant, in those intelligence reports." I commented.

"Neither do I." A.J. jumped in.

"Well we sure as hell better find out." Willie blurted out. "I, for one, would sure as hell hate to have that kind of surprise sprung on us once we're in there."

"Me too." A.J. said. "I'll have the colonel get us some info on that this afternoon."

"John, have Ray and Skip bring those other charts in here and lets see how they compare to these photos."

"Roger."

"Larry what explosives you think we'll need to blow this thing?" A.J. asked.

"Well, if the air strikes haven't penetrated this concrete barrier, nothing we can use on the outside is going to do much damage either." Larry replied. "We're going to have to, if we want complete destruction, blow it from the inside."

"Damn, I was afraid of that." Came A.J.'s reply. "That means that we'll have all that damn gas going off on us, and there's no telling what kind of bullshit gas their making there."

"Nah, maybe not." Larry came back.

"Why?"

"Well, Doug isn't it true that the finished product, the gas, that's the poison, and the ingredients shouldn't really hurt you?" Larry was looking to Doug for input.

"For the most part that's true. But a lot depends on what they're using and making."

"Well, depending on what's there, we could blow the surroundings and use a timer on the finished product. They're going to be busy running around to check for a timed delay."

"Sounds to me that a lot depends on how volatile the ingredients are and the proximity of the finished product." Alan interjected.

"Yeah." A.J. said as he reached for the charts that Skip and Ray had brought into the room, and laid them out in front of us to see. "What do these charts show us Ray?"

Ray and Skip began to show what they interpreted each placement was and what each placement probably did. It took the rest of the day, going through each detail of the charts and comparing various details with the photos. Trying to find a big chink in their armor was tough, however, we came up with a couple little ones that would give us the opening we needed. Now came the tedious work of planning every detail of the mission.

As Larry began to figure what explosives were needed to destroy the various components of the plant, the rest of us were assigned the different tasks each of us would be responsible for. We would have twenty five to thirty Iranians assigned to us and those would be broken down into five squads. Two of us would lead four of the squads and A.J. and their leader would lead the fifth, also each squad would have to accomplish two different tasks.

"A.J. we're going to need four birds for this." I declared. "I'll fly one then we'll need to use their pilots for the other three."

"Yeah, that's what I figured too," A.J. responded, "and that means a lot of work and risk hiding that many birds while we do the mission."

"Well if we come in here," Alan said as he pointed to a spot on the map that was about seven to ten miles to the east of the plant, "It looks like enough room to camouflage the birds and leave the three Iranian pilots with them, now, lets see, we'll be only about a hundred yards from the river here. So we take rafts and paddle up stream to here. We hide the rafts go in and after we're done we float back to the birds."

"I don't know. That river is pretty swift. Everything sounds good except I think we ought to walk to the plant along the river, then use the rafts on the way back." A.J. said.

"Anybody figure out how much moonlight we're going to have?" Ray asked.

"There is suppose to be about three quarters of a moon." A.J. came back. "That should be plenty. But we're going to need about six rafts and that's also a lot to hide."

"Not really." Doug interjected. "Once we're there, we're going to start so much chaos for them their not going to go looking for anything."

"That's true." A.J. shrugged. "Shit it's already dark, lets knock off for the night and finish up in the morning."

The plan was finalized and a run through was done with the Iranians over the week end. Now during the early morning hours of Monday, we were again at the airfield, preparing for our departure. A.J. had our team and the Iranian squad leaders gathered in front of the hanger, briefing them for the last time. I had taken the pilots of the other three helicopters to the back of the hanger and briefed them one last time on the flight plans and route.

"John, you about ready?" A.J. inquired.

175

"Roger." I answered as I was sending the pilots to their respective helicopters.

"Hey pal," Alan had joined me as I walked to the helicopter. "Let me have a cigarette, will ya. I don't know what the hell I did with mine."

"Sure, no problem." I responded handing him a cigarette and lighting one myself. "You ain't going goofy are you?"

"Hell no. I just lost my cigarettes. Ok?" He shrugged.

A.J. already had all the troops aboard the aircraft as Alan and I arrived and climbed in the helicopter. "We all set A.J.?" I asked.

"We're as ready as we're going to get with this gaggle. So lets go." He replied.

I turned on the main fuel and squeezed the trigger, starting the helicopter engine. This was also the signal for the other pilots to do the same. Bringing the RPMs up to operating speed, I pressed my mike button and began to broadcast, "Ok, from now on we are under radio silence. We take off in three minutes." The airways fell quiet once again.

The colonel didn't come out to the aircraft this time. He stood at the hanger door with his counter part, but still gave us his usual half salute. I nodded my head to him, pulled up on the collective and we were off.

We once again used Bakhtaran as a refueling point then continued on to point alpha. This mission, point alpha was a spot about ten miles down river from the gas plant. We landed there just as the fading sun began to cast its spell of darkness. Quickly we set about the task of concealing the aircraft and unloading all our gear. Soon darkness had set in enough for us to start our ten mile trek along the river bank to the plant. A.J. held one last minute briefing with the other pilots. A couple other men were left behind to guard the helicopters and act as our look outs upon our return, then we were marching off.

Arriving at the plant about a half past midnight, we swiftly stashed the inflatable rafts, which would be used for our get away, near the river's edge then assembled around A.J. "Alright it's O O thirty seven. I want the first charges going off at O two hundred. Everyone knows where you go and what to do so lets do it."

Alan and I gathered the Iranian squad assigned to us and headed for the main gate. First we headed west then north to the northwest corner of the plant where the main gate was located. Upon our arrival Alan and I signaled for our followers to halt and remain where they were. Seeing only two guards at the gate Alan and I edged closer to survey the area and saw no one else near by. Alan pointed to me and nodded his head to the left then pointed to himself and nodded to the right. I nodded in agreement and raised my nine millimeter, with its silencer attached, taking aim at the guard on the left. Almost in unison our weapons spit out metal projectiles with a psst, psst, and both guards fell silently to the ground.

Alan raised his arm signaling the rest to follow. We made our way to the gate and through it. I signaled for the bodies to be drug aside and posted two of our own in their place. The rest scurried to take their positions around the two large barracks that housed the guards and other personnel. I looked at my watch then signaled Alan that we had thirty five minutes to wait. He nodded and signaled the squad to set the charges, we had, around the barracks. This task took only about fifteen minutes. Now we must quietly wait and hope no one came by.

As it neared O two hundred hours, I raised my arm in the air. Any second now the fireworks would start. BOOM! Came the first explosion from the east side of the plant. I flung my arm down to my side and immediately both barracks became engulfed in an inferno of flames. A few survivors of the blast began to stumble from the fiery building and were gunned down by the men positioned outside. Explosions were now going off all over and the sky was no longer black. You could hear the rat a tat tat of gunfire coming from the main part of the plant as Alan started yelling to our squad and circling his hand over head. Swiftly the squad gathered and we retraced our route back to the river.

Arriving back at the river Alan and I immediately started popping the CO2 cartridges on the rafts, inflating them all. I was tossing paddles into each raft as the other squads began arriving. Alan placed a raft in the water and we filled it to capacity, jumped in ourselves and began paddling down river. Soon there was a train of rafts behind us.

The current was so swift it didn't take much effort to keep up a good speed. Even after seven or eight minutes down river, blasts could still be heard coming from the plant, then came the largest kaboom. The main blast had gone off, surely there wouldn't be much left of that place now.

Before long I spotted the signal from the look outs we left behind and we headed for shore. While Alan helped guide the other rafts behind us to shore I ran to the aircraft. The pilots had already uncovered the helicopters and had them in position to leave. I told them to start their birds then wait for me to lift off. Once I was up they were to do the same in the order I gave them. I climbed in the helicopter and got the rotor turning at flight speed and the other pilots did the same. A.J. and Alan were directing everyone to their assigned aircraft, and I knew that when they boarded, we would be all ready to leave. A.J. and Alan jumped in yelling "GO!" and I pulled the aircraft up into the air before they were even fastened in.

Once again I was landing back at the airfield but this time with three other helicopters behind me and after a successful mission. I sat the bird down on the ground and shut down the engine as the colonel walked toward us.

"Fine job boys." He said. "Let these guys take care of everything here and you guys get on the bus."

"I'm for that." Alan said.

The colonel smiled and continued, "We'll have our debriefing back at the compound and in the morning we'll head for home."

"All right!" I exclaimed.

CHAPTER 45

"Hey pal, ya think you might want to go fishing when we get back?" Alan asked me.

"Are you crazy? We spend more than half our time now out in nature." I answered as I turned my attention, from watching out the plane's window, to him.

"Yeah, maybe I am. But there's just something different about fishing. Hey you remember that little place up in Colorado I took you to? Now that wasn't that bad, was it?"

A broad grin came across my face as I answered, "Yeah I remember, and it wasn't a bad place at all. Maybe, we're both just crazy."

"Maybe so. So what do you think?"

"Oh, what the hell. A few more days of fresh air won't kill us I don't guess. Yeah ok."

We landed in Miami about mid morning, where the van met us and whisked us to the safe house. I walked straight through the front door and back to the bar. After fixing both Alan and myself a stiff scotch I announced, "Hey A.J., I need some go go powder."

As he tossed me his vile of cocaine, "What's the matter, you out?"

"Yeah, I need some more. You might as well get us both a little extra too."

"I'll do it this afternoon." A.J. came back. "What you need extra for? You guys got something going?"

"Yeah, dickhead here wants to go up to Colorado fishing." I chuckled.

"Fishing?" A.J. blurted out.

"Yeah, fishing!" Alan retorted. "Hey it's peaceful and relaxing. Ok?"

179

"Ok, ok." A.J. laughed. "I'll have it for you this afternoon."

"Thanks." I said as I snorted a large line of the white powder and handed the vile to Alan. "You know Alan, I would like to make a short stop though, on the way."

"Oh yeah, where?" He answered as he poured himself out a line of cocaine.

"Well, just one or two days. I'd kinda like to see my kids. You know?"

"Shit yeah man. No problem. We'll just make a stop for a couple of days there first. It's on the way anyhow."

"You guys just keep me informed of where you are, in case something comes up." A.J. interjected.

"Yeah, we know the routine." I answered.

Alan and I got our things together that afternoon and left that night for Texas. We spent two days there while I raveled about how big my two sons had gotten, then went on to Colorado. After five days of what Alan thought was peaceful and I thought was miserable, I told him, "Alan, I've had about all this nature shit I can stand."

Laughing he said, "Oh alright. What you want to do?"

"Hell I don't know. Guess just go back to Miami. A.J. said last night that something should be coming up soon."

"You want to leave tonight or in the morning?" He asked.

"Morning's fine."

"That's great with me. Damn though, I was beginning to think you wouldn't ever say 'lets get out of here' and I sure as hell wasn't going to be the first to say it."

"You son of a bitch!" I laughed.

We flew back to Miami where we basked on the beach and sucked in the rays of the sun for the next week and a half. Finally the colonel announced we had a mission and he would hold a briefing the next morning.

"Alright guys," The colonel began. "We're going back to the far east."

"We going in after the Americans held captive?" I asked with anticipation.

"No John, I'm still working on that, believe me."

"Yeah." I sighed.

"We're going back to Thailand. The Laotian and Cambodians are still trying to invade there. Our job is going to be to try to slow them down a little." The colonel continued on without going back to the subject of the Americans. "There's three major areas we want to hit. For right now, however, we're only dealing with one. That's a place called Pakse in Laos. They've got a big troop build up there and they keep sending raids across the boarder to hit the base at Ubon."

"When we leaving sir?" Alan asked.

"The day after tomorrow. A.J. here's got all the planning material you're going to need, so between now and then, you can get ready. You will go to Bangkok to finish your preparation then on to Ubon. Any other questions?"

"Yes sir." I spoke up. "While we're over there anyway, why in the hell not just get the Americans too?"

"Cause John, first, you know the area where you saw them is quite a bit north of where you're going now. Second, you know by now, the government has to approve everything and till we get their ok, there's nothing more we can do. Believe me, I understand how you feel, I also feel for them, there is just nothing I can do right now. Ok, if there's nothing else lets break this briefing up and you guys get started on planning."

"Yeah, I understand." I mumbled as Alan and I headed to the bar.

Alan fixed us a drink while I poured out a couple lines of cocaine. After snorting my large line, I handed the tray to Alan, took my drink and said, "Alan, why in the hell are we in this?"

"I don't know, why?"

"Why in the hell do we risk our lives for everyone else? There ain't anyone who really gives a damn about us. There never has been and probably never will be."

"Yeah pal, I think you're right, but what the hell else are we going to do? And the money ain't bad."

"Bullshit Alan! You know we don't give a shit about the money. In fact I don't know if I give a shit about anything anymore."

"Hey, I know pal, I feel the same way, but it ain't going to do us any good to sit here crying about the way the world is."

"Hey you guys." A.J. interrupted. "You want to come in here and lets get started on this."

"Yeah. On our way." I responded shaking my head.

The rest of the day and all the next, we went over the plans of what we were to do and the maps. The plan was pretty simple, real dangerous but simple. Then the third day we boarded a plane. Bangkok here we come, ready or not.

CHAPTER 46

Thoughts of the captive Americans, left behind from the Vietnam War, drifted through my mind as the plane touched down at Dong Mong airport in Thailand. For some reason, maybe because of my own captivity, I couldn't get these discarded men out of my mind. Maybe I felt spurned and forgotten myself by the American public and felt the need to remember these real patriots, or maybe I just wanted the American public to see how evil and inhumane I thought they were.

"Earth to John." Alan's words brought me back to reality. "You alright?'

"Yeah." I responded.

"Well lets go, they're all waiting on us."

We left the plane and were escorted around customs and on to a military van. The van made its way across the airport to MACV, the military side of the airport. Here we were greeted by an Army major who showed us the little section we were being allowed to have exclusive access to. He also explained that we already had rooms down town at the Chopia Hotel and the exclusive use of the van and driver.

"If there is anything that you may need, here is how you can reach me twenty four hours a day." The major said handing A.J. a piece of paper. "Now I don't know what your function or job here is," He continued, "but I'm not stupid. Orders and clearance for you came from pretty high up and I just want you to know that I have a top-secret clearance and if I can be of any help to you in anyway, just call."

"Thank you sir." A.J. graciously responded. "Right now however, I think we're just going to go to the hotel for the night."

I chuckled to myself as the van driver weaved his way through the city of daredevil drivers, to the hotel, "These people are something else. Aren't they." I quipped.

"That they are pal, that they are." Alan agreed.

The next morning we all met at the hotel restaurant for breakfast. We hurriedly consumed our food and then boarded the van. The driver once again weaved his way through the streets to the airport and to the, now restricted to everyone but us, office. The next two days were spent going over the maps and our plan, and acquiring what little equipment we were getting. The only major item we were to pick up here was the helicopter, all the destructive gear and armament we would get when we reached Ubon.

"Alright guys." A.J. said. "Everything's ready here. Lets go back to the hotel for the night and we leave at O seven hundred tomorrow."

In Ubon we spent the day organizing the cashe of armament we were given. Each of us would carry a large amount of satchel charges and booby traps in addition to our M16 rifles, pistols and other standard items we always carried. That night we would leave for Laos.

Pakse, Laos was only about one hundred and twenty miles from Ubon and about fifty to fifty five miles from the Thai boarder. It was too risky to take the helicopter all the way to Pakse. Besides part of our mission was the route to Pakse, so we had arranged to land at a small site just short of the boarder, where a company of Thai soldiers would guard the helicopter till our hopeful return. We would walk the last fifty five or so miles.

I landed the helicopter at the designated site and the Thai soldiers immediately encircled the aircraft. While the troops were securing the aircraft we unloaded our gear and strapped on our overstuffed packs. The one good thing about the packs was that they would get lighter as we went along.

"Ok guys." A.J. began. "I think we're ready. Break down into the three groups, (the three groups consisted of - myself, Alan, Ray - Charlie, Willie, Doug - A.J., Skip, Larry) make sure you each have your maps and lets head out to your assigned routes."

No one spoke a word, just nodded as Alan, Ray and myself headed for our assignment route. Each group would take a different route to Pakse, the routes were heavily traveled enemy troop trails. On the trek to Pakse each group would plant land mines and booby traps along the way at pinpoint locations depicted on the map. None of these would be armed however, that would be done on the way back. We accomplished our placements and arrived at the rendezvous point late afternoon the next day. Doug, Charlie and Willie were already there however the other three hadn't shown yet.

"Hey, how long you been here?" I asked.

"Oh, bout twenty minutes." Charlie answered.

"Shit, that's pretty good timing." Alan stated. "Ya have any trouble?"

"Nah, not really." Doug came back. "We had to duck a couple patrols but they're so damn dumb they wouldn't know anything anyway. What about you guys?"

I chuckled at Doug's comment and said, "We didn't see a soul."

A.J. and the other two scampered toward us and A.J. said, "Damn, those son of bitches are all over out there."

"Shit, you must of had the main trail then, cause none of us had any trouble." Ray responded.

"I didn't say we had any trouble, I just said there was a lot of those son a bitches out there." A.J. snapped back. "Everyone get all their plants in?"

We all nodded in the affirmative then A.J. continued, "Ok, we'll rest here till dark then go in and plant the charges at their base camp."

We all pulled out some of our rations and ate the cold food. After I finished my beans and weenies I threw the tin can in the whole that was dug to hide our trash and reached in my pocket for my vile of cocaine. Taking a couple snorts the weariness left my body and I was ready for anything.

It wasn't long before the shadows began to creep across the jungle and soon the night sounds of the jungle flourished. The jungle became very dark at night, sometimes you couldn't even see the sky at all.

"Alright, lets go." A.J. commanded.

No response was required as we grabbed our now semi-light packs and scurried off. When we arrived at the base camp of our enemy, A.J. began pointing out our directions and sending us to our assigned tasks. Slithering along the ground we cut our way through the barbwire parameter and off in different directions. I swiftly planted the charges in my designated places and set the timers for thirty minutes.

I had just finished planting my last charge and began to crawl to my exit, when a shot rang out. "Oh shit." I thought as I jerked my head toward the origin of the gunfire. Three soldiers were standing, still pointing their rifles at a figure on the ground. The figure was one of us. With no time for thinking, I squeezed the trigger of my M16, empting the clip into the soldiers and they fell lifeless to the ground. I quickly ran to the figure, OH NO, OH NO, it was Alan.

"Where you hit?" I asked.

"The back." He groaned.

"How bad?"

"Bad."

"Bullshit! It ain't bad." I tried to scoff. "You've had worse, come on, grab on."

Just then Doug appeared and could see I was trying to drag Alan to safety. Grabbing his other arm, he said, "Lets get the hell out a here."

We scurried to the parameter and under the fence as the hustle and bustle began to build behind us. Just as we reached the rendezvous point, the first charge went off. Boom, boom, boom, one right after another and I knew that their entire camp was now in complete turmoil.

"How bad is he?" A.J. asked me.

I just looked at him and he knew that I thought it was bad. "Damn," He said. "Alright we got to get out of here guys, and make sure everything's armed on your way."

I grabbed A.J.'s arm and said, "I ain't leaving him A.J."

"Damn John, you know the game. We got a mission to complete."

"I ain't leaving him!" I snapped.

"I'll help with him." Ray added.

"Oh alright." A.J. answered. "But you guys make sure you get all the plants armed and we ain't waiting more than an hour back at the bird. Understand?"

"Yeah." I sneered.

Doug jumped in, "I'll break off and go with John and Ray, Willie and Charlie can handle the route we had."

"Ok, ok, but lets get the hell out of here." A.J. commanded.

I grabbed Alan's arm and pulled it around my neck and Ray grabbed the other arm. As soon as we reached the trail, Ray said, "Hey Doug you help John, I'll do the arming."

"No." I came back as I yanked off my belt. "You guys do the arming, I'll handle Alan."

"Sure?"

I nodded yes as I tied Alan's arms around my neck. Then hoisting him up and grabbing his legs about my sides, I now had him piggy back.

By morning my legs began to cramp, but there was no way I was going to set Alan down. My mind drifted back to when he shared his measly portions of rations with me because mine were taken away in the POW camp. Oh God, we had been through a lot together, "you can't die now." I kept repeating to myself.

While the other two were arming the booby traps I took a short rest and inhaled a large dose of cocaine. Instantly I felt somewhat rejuvenated and once again off we went.

We reached the Thai boarder close to noon and as the mined trail ended, the rest of the team met us. Skip, Larry and Charlie grabbed Alan off my back then Doug and Ray took my arms. As they began to hustle us off for the last few miles, to the helicopter, I turned to A.J. and said, "Thanks man."

"Oh what the hell. Come on." He responded.

Arriving at the helicopter we quickly scrambled aboard and I had us in the air in a flash. I radioed Dong Mong airport and told them to have an ambulance meet us, then nosed the helicopter over and red lined it (went maximum speed) back to Bangkok, not stopping at Ubon.

CHAPTER 47

Alan had been in surgery for over five hours. We jumped to our feet as the attendants wheeled him out. I dashed over and asked, "How is he doc?"

"I think he's going to be alright." The doctor said as he took off his mask.

"Oh God!" I sighed and a big grin came to the whole team.

The doctor continued, "They are taking him to recovery right now and he'll be out for awhile, but you can probably see him in the morning."

"Why can't I sit with him now?" I asked.

"Well no one is allowed in the recovery room." He said.

"He's going to be ok John." A.J. said as he put his arm on my shoulder. "Come on, I'll buy you a drink, I think we both need one. Hell, we all need one, come on I'm buying."

I was at the hospital every day, all day for the next five days, while we waited for our next mission. Alan was alert and able to get up and move around for short periods of time. On the first day Alan tried to thank me but neither of us had the right words for our emotions. No words were needed, however, we both knew how the other felt.

Mid-morning of the sixth day I was sitting in Alan's room, drinking coffee, when A.J. came strolling in, "Hey how you feeling Alan?"

"Fine." He replied.

"Great. You talk to the doc today?" A.J. asked.

"Not today yet." Alan answered.

"What's up?" I asked.

"We got orders." A.J. came back. "We're suppose to scrub the rest of the mission here and head back to Miami immediately."

"What's the big happening?" I inquired.

"Don't know, but whatever it is, it's big." A.J. said then looked at Alan and asked, "You think they'll let you travel?"

"I don't know about going on a job," Alan spoke with a half laugh, "but I feel good enough to travel."

"I know you're not going on a job for awhile." A.J. answered with a grin. "Come on John, lets find the doc and see what he says."

The doctor agreed to let Alan travel as long as he used a wheelchair and didn't walk too much for the next several days. That evening we all boarded a plane, going back to Miami. After a long flight and a change of planes in New York we arrived back at the safe house where the colonel was waiting for us.

"Hi ya boys." He greeted us. "How you feeling Alan?"

"Fine sir fine."

"Great, great. Come on in here, I'll let all of you relax in a minute, but first come here." He said leading us to the meeting room. "Ok boys we're not sure what we're going to do yet, but we're going to do something. Ayatollah Khomeini has overthrown the Shah of Iran."

"Who the hell is this Ayatollah Ka—whatever?" I asked.

"I guess he used to be in charge there a long time ago or something like that and he's been in exile. At any rate he sure doesn't like us. They overran the embassy there and took everyone hostage. All hell is breaking out over there."

"Jesus!" I commented.

"What they going to have us do sir? This sounds like military action to me." A.J. responded.

"Well it normally would be, but our wimpy assed president probably ain't going to do anything, he ain't got any balls at all, so you can bet your ass we'll be in it somehow. I should know more tomorrow or the next day. You guys just stay ready."

That night we all set around discussing what we might be used for and coming up with all kinds of wild ideas. "Maybe they're going to have us take out this Ayatollah guy." I said as I snorted a large line of cocaine.

"Hey John, fix me a line, will ya?" Alan asked.

"What, you know the doc said you ain't suppose to have this stuff. You ain't even suppose to have that drink there." I said.

"Come off it will ya. You know doctors don't know shit." He retorted.

"Oh ok."

"I doubt if they would have us try to hit this guy, or anyone else for that matter, after that Sadahm fiasco." A.J. said and we all laughed.

The next evening the colonel announced he was catching a flight for Nellis Air force Base in Nevada. "You fellows will leave here tomorrow afternoon to join me."

"Colonel, isn't Nellis by Las Vegas?" I asked.

"Yeah it is." He nodded.

"Alright." Alan said.

"First off," The colonel came back, "Alan, you ain't going, and as for the rest of you, I doubt you'll have much time for Vegas. Now I'm leaving, make sure you're on that flight tomorrow."

"Yeah," Alan added, "and you guys better be damn careful, since I won't be there to take care of your asses."

"Look who needs taken care of." I said causing the whole room to laugh.

CHAPTER 48

After arriving at Nellis Air force Base in the early evening, we were taken to the bachelor officer quarters. There, Colonel Myers met us and assigned a room to each of us. "Now, you boys take your things upstairs to your room and meet me back down here directly." He told us as the sergeant behind the desk was issuing keys. In a matter of moments we were gathered around the colonel. "Alright boys, first let me say, we're not sure on what direction we're taking on this one yet. However, the brass has got a couple avenues we're looking at and I can tell you right now even though they have started a diplomatic angle, it won't work. Also, I'm sure they haven't got the balls for any military action, so you all can be sure you're going to be involved. We're pulling in, to here, eight other teams and have a few more on standby. I don't know if they've all arrived yet, but we've got a briefing tomorrow at eleven hundred hours at the four thirty third squadron hanger, its been cleared and as of this morning, it is for our use only. Now I'm sure you don't know where it's located, so we'll meet here at ten thirty hours in the morning and I'll take you over there. Now then, I'm sure you already know this but, this is a closed base, and access is restricted. I've got temporary pass cards here that I'll give you in just a minute. They'll get you on and off the base. Don't loose them! Cause you're also going to need them to have access to the hanger. Everyone understand?"

"Yes sir." Everyone acknowledged.

"Sir," I asked, "I presume this means we'll be allowed to go into town."

"Yes, I'm coming to that now. First, you will be, like always, be required to be at every scheduled briefing, but if we have nothing for you, you're free to do whatever. However, you are on one hour alert call, which means, wherever you go you have to be able to be back here within one hour. I have pagers, one for each of you. You will keep it with you at all times and I do mean at all times, even if you're in bed with some broad." He paused while everyone chuckled. "If you're paged and the numbers come up all nines, that's the code for you to assemble at the hanger immediately. There's going to be other codes but you'll get them tomorrow. That's about all I have for now, once you have your pass cards and pager you're free to do whatever."

"Sir, one thing," Doug spoke up as the colonel was passing out the cards and pagers, "you think there would be a chance of getting some money? I left almost all mine back in Miami."

"Oh yeah." The colonel said reaching into another compartment of his briefcase. "Here, I got five thousand dollars for each of you. If you need more see me tomorrow and I'll see what I can do."

We all were issued our card, pager and cash and the colonel began to leave as I asked, "What's everyone going to do?" I felt at a loss not having Alan around to team up with.

Everyone had their own ideas of what they were going to do except A.J. and I. A.J. didn't go in much for the carousing, like the rest of our team, so he suggested, "Since you haven't got anything special, why don't we just go into town and see what's happening. I don't really want to stay long but I'm sure I can throw a few bucks away."

"Sounds alright to me." I answered. "Let me just run upstairs and get some pep (cocaine) then we'll see about catching a cab."

A.J. went back to the base early, but I was on a winning streak playing twenty one. At around eight o'clock in the morning I was ahead a little over four thousand dollars and figured it was a good time to quit. I flipped the dealer a black chip (worth a hundred dollars), went to breakfast, took a couple snorts of cocaine and went back to the base.

For the next two weeks we had a briefing almost every day, but not much ever came out of them. The one thing that did, was my thankfulness that I was on the team I was on. Almost everyone on the other teams seemed real strange and some even weird. Sometimes I wondered if they thought the same about me. There was one thing for sure though, no matter how strange or weird I thought they were, I knew they knew their jobs and were real good at it.

Before long we were told that the diplomatic angle wasn't going anywhere (oh gee, what a surprise) and it looked like it was our turn. We were also told that we had real good intelligence reports on where all the hostages were being kept. Now what we needed to do was come up with a way to get them out safely.

The hanger began to come alive, as every day a group of us mauled through the reports, looking for a way to get the hostages out. I was amazed to find out that most of the other teams did not do their own planning. When they were given a mission they were also told how to do it. Gradually an idea began to blossom and all the team heads (Colonel Myers etc.) gathered the bits together. Then they told us that the rest of the planning would be done by them. The rest of us were now just on alert, no briefings or anything, till we were paged.

"Hello." The voice responded into the phone.

"Hey Alan, what's up." I asked.

"Hey pal, how ya doing? Guess you've been having too much fun and night life to think about your old pal back here, half bored to death, huh."

"Shit, you think you're bored you ought to be here."

"I will be." Alan came back.

"What'da you mean?" I asked.

"Well, I talked to the colonel yesterday and he's arranging it for me to be out there day after tomorrow."

"Great. But what the hell you going to do? You can't go on a job yet."

"Hell I don't know, but he said he'd find something for me. Hell anything's better than just sitting around here."

"That's about all you'll do here. We haven't even had a briefing in the last three and a half weeks.

"Well, we'll find something to do. I hear the women in Vegas are something else and besides I'll probably end up getting rich." Alan responded laughing.

"Yeah right." I answered. "So I'll see you in a couple days, right?"

"Roger that."

Alan's arrival made the waiting a little more bearable. We spent the next four days, and most of the nights, going from casino to casino and neither of us getting any richer. It was amazing to me, however, how much more fun everything was when you had your best, and probably only true, friend sharing it with you.

Finally the pager sang out. Beep, beep, beep. I looked down at it and seven nines appeared. "Well it looks like we got something." I said as Alan's pager was also now beeping. Grabbing the stack of chips in front of me, "You cash in all these chips and I'll go out front and get us a cab." I said handing Alan my chips.

I told the doorman I had an emergency and needed a cab quick. He waved his arm and a cab came pulling up to me. He opened the back door for me, I handed him a five dollar bill and said to the taxi driver, "We got to wait just a second for my friend. How long will it take you to get us out to Nellis?"

"The airbase, oh, with the traffic tonight, about thirty five, forty minutes." He answered.

As Alan was getting in on the other side, I said, "Tell you what partner, I got a hundred dollar bill here if you can get us there in twenty."

"You're on."

When we arrived at the hanger, we showed our pass cards and were told to find our team leader. Alan spotted Colonel Myers along the back wall with A.J. "Here we are." I said holding out my arms from my sides as we walked up to them. "Where's everyone else?"

"Doug and Skip just went over to the BOQ (bachelor officer quarters), the rest should be here anytime." A.J. said.

"Alright, here's what we got." The colonel took over. "We're going in after the hostages. You're to stay on base from now on, we got a briefing in the morning at O nine hundred and bring all your things cause we leave for Saudi at thirteen hundred."

"What about me sir? You want me on the mission too?" Alan asked.

"As of now you're my assistant. You can't go on the mission but there's a lot you can do to help everyone get ready for it. Now, you boys go on over to the BOQ and I'll see you in the morning."

CHAPTER 49

The hair dryer type breeze, that met us as we disembarked the airplane in Saudi Arabia, reminded me of the last time we were in this area. That time however, we were helping Iran, this time we were enemies. "Things can change so fast." I thought.

We were herded on to a couple large buses and driven to a small landing strip area with several large buildings. Two of the buildings were set up to house all of us, and unlike quarters we were normally given, these buildings had no rooms. They were just two large open buildings with cots lined up and down both sides. Another building was set up to accommodate the team heads. Needless to say their accommodations were a little better than ours. The landing strip also had two very large aircraft hangers and in a portion of one of them a briefing area was set up.

After exiting the buses, "Everyone find yourself a bunk, put your things up and then assemble in that hanger over there." One of the team heads told us pointing to the hanger with the briefing area set up.

Our team, as did most of the other teams, took cots together in a group. Throwing the lone bag I was carrying on a cot, I took out my vile of cocaine, took a huge snort, to get rid of the jet lag that was already setting in, and said, "I don't know about you guys, but I sure could go for some grub."

"Me too." Skip agreed.

"Yeah, I bet they pass out some God dam C rations after a briefing." Alan said.

"I wouldn't doubt it." A.J. joined in. "Come on guys lets head on over to the hanger."

As we walked into the hanger I looked at Alan and began to laugh, cause sitting right there was a pallet of C rations. "See I told you." Alan said.

"Alright, alright." Colonel Myers said getting everyone's attention. "I'm going to go over a few rules first then I'll give you the basic plan. First, the Saudi government doesn't normally like having foreign troops in their country, however they have agreed to allow us to stage this rescue from here. While here, we are their guests and we'll conduct ourselves as such, that means you will observe all their rules and customs. However you won't have a chance not to, cause you will not leave this facility at all unless told to do so. Is that understood?" The colonel took a short pause even though there was no response from his audience. "Also tomorrow there will be a company of Saudi troops here. They will be setting up some mock ups on the east side for us. Leave them alone! I don't even want you out there. Understood?" Another pause and silence. "Now then, here's our basic plan, we'll get into lot more detail over the next several days." He continued on as he pulled up the cover draped over a large board to reveal a big map, and with his pointer, "Here, these red dots represent where the hostages are being held. We know the exact location of all of them and how many are at each location. Basically what we're going to do is, we'll rendezvous a C one thirty (airplane) and nine UH-1H helicopters out here in the desert. From there the helicopters will take the teams, and right here let me say, we're going to try and keep the teams together as much as possible, but some of you may be split up. Ok, the helicopters will take the teams from here to here, here, here, and here. You will then proceed to the location assigned to you, retrieve the hostages at that location and return them to the helicopters, then back to the C one thirty which will take the hostages off and you will make your exit. Now all this sounds pretty basic and simple, but it's not. The timing has got to be perfect, all the hostages have got to be retrieved at the same time. As we get into this plan you'll see that everything has got to be done precisely when and how the plan dictates." The colonel went on for about another ten or fifteen minutes then, just like Alan had predicted, we were given C rations. We were also told we would begin our in depth look at the plan at thirteen hundred the next day and start running through it the day after that, when the mock ups were completed.

At the thirteen hundred hours briefing we were divided into groups and assigned which hostages we would be responsible for. The night before the colonel had asked me if I wanted to pilot one of the helicopters or be in one of the groups, "Hell, I guess I might as well get in on the real action, I'll be in one of the groups." I told him.

The man conducting the briefing sure didn't look the part of a team head or anything like it. He looked like he should be behind a desk somewhere, doing some accounting. I figured that he was some genius that Washington sent but wondered if he was something other than he looked. "Each group has a detailed map of the entire area you are assigned." He began to explain. "The reason you have that map is so you can study it and know every house, street, alley, every little detail of that area. We are getting real good intelligence on all this, however, they move the hostages from house to house every few days to keep us off guard."

Over the next eight days we worked in our small group and everyone as a whole, going over every little point and contingency. We had briefing after briefing after briefing and then ran through everything in the mock up area. We spent twelve to fourteen hours a day crossing every T and dotting every I. It was really starting to take shape now, and everyone had confidence in it working.

"Lets go over everything again men, cause it looks like we got a mission date. Wednesday. Two days from now."

CHAPTER 50

The busyness picked up. Equipment was being checked and loaded on the aircraft. Little details were worked out and as lift off time neared we became more and more anxious.

"Briefing in one hour." Word came.

"Relax men, I got some disheartening news. The mission date has been delayed." The team head conducting the briefing paused as groans filled the room. "Hold on, hold on, let me finish. The word we got is that the President is having second thoughts, however, everyone thinks he'll go through with it. So the mission date will only be probably delayed a couple days, and we can use that time to refine everything. Take the rest of the day off and relax, we'll start again right here in the morning at O nine hundred." Everyone left the briefing area grumbling and mumbling obscenities.

"Why in the hell does our government get people to sacrifice for them, then just discard them?" I asked as Alan, A.J. and I walked back to our billets.

"Beats the hell out of me." Alan said.

"You can bet your ass that they won't forget these." A.J. said. "There's too much publicity already out there to sweep this one under the rug."

"Yeah, what the hell happened to the publicity about the poor son of a bitch in Vietnam?" I asked.

"Shit John, wake up. The American people themselves were against the Vietnam soldier. What the hell would publicity do, other than make them hate us more." Alan stated.

When we reached our cots, we snorted come cocaine and opened a beer. Beer was the only type of booze we could get here and that was even hard to come by. We continued to talk, snort cocaine, and drink beer most of the night. We finally came to the conclusion that some lives were just worth more than others and ours, as Vietnam veterans were worthless. Oh what a great country we had.

The next few days we worked on refining the plan till it could be refined no more. There was no doubt on anyone's part that we could pull this off in our sleep. Now, all we needed was for someone to say "Do it".

"If we don't do something pretty soon, I'm going to run out of this go powder." Alan said as we both inhaled a line of cocaine.

"Yeah, me too. Wonder if A.J. can get us more while we're here?" I answered.

"Hey everyone, immediate briefing, right now." A.J. said as he came in panting. "Lets get over there, this could be it."

We all eagerly jumped to our feet and hurried to the briefing hanger. Everyone quickly took their seats and became quiet, awaiting Colonel Myers, already standing in front, to speak.

"Well men." He began with a sigh, and I knew what he was about to say wasn't what we wanted to hear. "It looks like we're not going on this one."

"Why not?" Someone yelled out.

"They just going to blow these guys off?" Someone else yelled.

"Wait a minute, wait a minute, let me tell you what's going to happen." He said holding up his hands signaling everyone to be quiet. "Some time early in the morning a military unit, from Fort Bragg, will be here. The President has decided to do this but to use the Army. Now we all have to help here. We're going to have two days to brief them and help them with everything we know."

"Jesus Christ, sir, you expect us to give them in two days everything we've done in, what, a month?" Someone asked.

"That's about it and whether we like it or not, that's the way it's going to be." The colonel answered.

The Army unit arrived and for the next two days we went through every phase of our plan. They were briefed on the latest intelligence and we gave them all our ideas on how we thought it should be handled. Most of our plans and ideas, they scoffed at however, because "they were trained for this sort of thing" and knew better than us. Soon they were loading up and leaving. We were scheduled to go home the next evening.

The night the Army unit left, most of us gathered at the briefing hanger. We were given permission to follow the progress of the rescue attempt and the team heads brought a radio in for us, even though there would be very little radio communications. It was hard to follow their progress however, because we were not given the unit's plan. Well after midnight they had an accident, a helicopter flew into a C one thirty, or something like that as best we could figure.

"Those stupid bastards." Alan said. "If their egos weren't so God Damn big they would've heard us tell them about flying in the sandy desert."

"Shh, shh." A.J. interrupted, causing us all to listen to the radio broadcast.

"Did you hear what I think I heard?" I asked.

"I think so." A.J. answered. "The son of bitches are canceling the mission and coming out."

"At least, even when we screwed up, we still got the mission done." I said.

"What happens now? It'll be hard to pull something off now since they'll be looking for it." Alan inquired.

"Shit, I don't know." A.J. said. "Lets go over and see if the colonel knows anything."

We walked over to the building that housed the team heads. We knew they were awake, as they had a command center set up in there and were also monitoring the progress of the mission. A.J. knocked on the door and asked for the colonel.

When he came to the door, "Did you hear what's going on sir?" A.J. asked.

"Yes, I heard. It's a shame, cause there are causalities and all for nothing." He answered.

"What happens now sir? Ya think they'll have us go in now?" I asked.

"No I don't think so. The President is too much of a whimp to do anything else. As far as I know we still go home tomorrow, well actually this evening. And I really don't think that will change." The colonel told us, and he was right. That coming evening we were on our way back to Miami.

CHAPTER 51

My eyes began to water as we sat around the TV at the Miami safe house, watching the Iranian hostages exiting the airplane. They were now free and back home, alive and well. My emotions ran rampant and it was impossible to tell which emotion was stronger. I felt great joy and happiness on the behalf of the hostages, knowing that feeling of once again being free. I also had a great resentment toward the cheering American public, giving the ex-hostages a hero's welcome. What did they do to deserve this welcome that the Vietnam veteran didn't do?

"What the hell you think this new President did to get them released?" A.J. ask the general question to the room.

"I don't know, but at least he did something, unlike his predecessor." I said standing to fix myself another scotch.

"Here, fix me one too, will ya?" Alan asked holding out his glass. "Look at all those damn people cheering, will ya." He continued and I knew he had the same feelings I had.

"Don't get me wrong here," I began, "but why do these guys get so much praise for just being captured and then released, when the Vietnam guy really sacrificed for the country gets shit on?"

"That's a different thing than this is." Skip stated.

"Bullshit!" Alan announced. "Why in the hell is it different?" He added as he accepted his fresh drink from me.

"Because, war was the job of the Vietnam soldier." Skip began. "And the press made us out like mongers and baby killers. What the hell was the public suppose to think of us?"

"The press made us out that way cause that's the way the public wanted to view us." I said.

"Well, there will never be a war like Vietnam again." A.J. said. "Even though I totally agree that we deserve a hell of a lot better treatment, you got to admit the way we fought that war was all screwed up."

"But that's not the point." Alan interjected.

"Sure it is Alan." A.J. came back. "We fought a passive war instead of an aggressive one. That created situations like Lieutenant Cowley, which fed the anti-war people."

The discussion went on, sometimes getting pretty heated, all night. Looking back on that night I should have noticed that everything was really building up inside Alan. He was starting to let all the mixture of emotions, that we both had, jam up inside him. Maybe there wasn't anyway to change what fate had in store for us, but I now wish I would have tried something.

We stayed in Miami for over a month waiting for another job to come along. During this time Alan and I both began to drink more and more, also our cocaine use increased. Several times, more than I wish to count, we were involved in fights in the local bars and night clubs. None of these places, however wanted to ban us because we spent so much money.

Finally the colonel called a briefing. "Boys we got another one we're not suppose to be in."

"Are we suppose to be in any of them?" Alan asked in a joking manner but I knew he was serious.

"I guess not." The colonel responded chuckling. "However, this one's a little different, it's in Nicaragua, and we won't be going in as a team on a specific mission. In fact it's going to split us up for awhile." He paused as he looked at our confused and inquisitive looks. "First of all we're short pilots, so John and Alan, you will be flying resupply missions. The rest of you will be on the ground, fighting alongside the other troops."

"Sir," A.J. spoke up, "does this mean we are disbanding this team?"

"Just temporally. I have been assured we will reassemble in a couple of months." The colonel answered. "However A.J. you're being moved up. You won't be going, instead you will be helping me coordinate different things."

"Does that mean more money?" A.J. joked, causing laughter to fill the room.

The colonel ignored A.J.'s comment and continued on explaining the different facets of the reorganization. He also explained that none of us had to accept this job and it would not jeopardize anything when the team reformed. All of us, however, immediately agreed to go.

"When's all this taking place?" Doug asked.

"Well as of right now A.J. you're going to help me, John and Alan, you guys will have to get checked out in the C one thirty, so I'm not sure about you yet. The rest of you will leave next week."

We all left the briefing glad that we were going to be doing something, but also with a sense of sadness about being broke up. As a team, we had come to know and accept the little quirks in each of us and cared deeply about each other.

A few days went by, then A.J. came to us, "Alright you guys are to be at the base in the morning. See Richardson there and he'll get you current in the C one thirty. Where you go from there and your flight schedule will be handled by someone there, and this will be the last chance I have to boss you around for awhile."

"Shit A.J. you ain't ever been able to boss us around before." Alan laughed.

"That ain't no shit." A.J. retorted.

For the next four days Alan and I had training flights in the C one thirty. I couldn't begin to count the number of landings, take-offs and simulated emergency procedures we practiced during that time, but I did rediscover that I did not like that plane. Soon we were on our way to Honduras. From there we would fly supplies and air drop them into Nicaragua.

Over the next few months we flew many missions into Nicaragua, the vast majority of which we weren't fired at. Rarely would we return with bullet holes in the aircraft and that was ok by me. Every few weeks we would be sent back to Miami for a four or five day R and R, however the main reason for being sent back, I think, was to carry a plane load of cocaine.

During this time Alan was becoming more and more introverted. He wasn't joking around like he used to just becoming lost in his own thoughts. Our little venting talks became less and less frequent till they became nonexistent. Our alcohol and cocaine use continued to increase however.

"Hey, you guys hear about Russell's plane today?" One of the other pilots asked as we were returning from our mission.

"No. What happened?" I asked.

"They got shot down." He told us.

"No shit. Where?"

"I think it was up in the mountain area just north of Matagalpa."

"Damn, did they make it out ok?" I continued to question.

"Doesn't look like it. I heard that there was only one survivor and he was captured."

"Who lived?" I again asked.

"I don't know, but I do know there's a bunch of tap dancing going on by the brass right now." He answered me.

CHAPTER 52

Everyone, on the plane shot down in Nicaragua, were killed except one of the cargo handlers. He had been taken captive and for the last two weeks confessed to being CIA. All hell was breaking loose and our government was denying any and all connections. Troops were being gathered and sent back to the states.

Alan and I were flying our last mission, taking a group of exiting fighting men back to Miami. I made the comment, "That poor son of a bitch. I wonder what will be done to get him out?" Referring to the downed cargo handler.

"Screw him." Alan said.

"What the hell do ya mean, Alan?" I curtly asked. "You know how it is to be in captivity."

"Bullshit. The stupid son of a bitch shouldn't be talking. He knew the game and the risks when he signed on." Alan snapped.

"Oh, come on Alan." I said. "You know what's done to get someone to say anything they want him to say. Did you forget where the hell we were and what they did to us?"

"I ain't forgot shit, but this asshole is different. The guy wasn't even in captivity two days before he started crying. We ought to send a team in and kill the bastard." Alan was explicitly saying. He was becoming so enraged about the subject I thought it better to just drop the discussion.

We landed in Miami, turned in the plane and other things then caught a cab to the safe house. We headed straight for the bar and were snorting a line of cocaine when A.J. entered the room, "Hey guys, great to see you."

"Yeah." Alan grumbled.

"I'm sure glad to be done with this one." I said with a big grin and a long pull from my glass of scotch.

"Well it looks like we'll be down for a while." A.J. came back.

"Why's that?" I asked.

"I think the company's going to have to lay low for awhile." A.J. said as Alan left saying he was going to his room.

"What's wrong with him?" A.J. asked me.

"Just tired I think." I said then went back to what we were talking about. "Why you say the company's going to lay low?"

"It seems that the word's out that we were funding the Nicaragua thing with funds from the sales of arms to Iran."

"You're shitting me. We were selling arms to Iran after all the bullshit we had a while back?" I asked with surprise.

"Yep. We were" He answered.

"Boy. Some brass is going to be, or I guess they already have been caught with their pants down." I commented.

"Yeah, and their dicks hanging out." A.J. laughed.

"What happens now?"

"Well," A.J. began as I raised my empty glass in a manner that was asking if he wanted one with me. He nodded yes and continued, "I guess everyone's suppose to lay low and not talk to anyone about anything. Who knows about later?"

"What about the rest of our guys?" I asked as I handed him a freshly mixed drink.

"They're on their way out now. They'll be here tomorrow or the next day."

A.J. and I continued to talk for the next couple of hours. I had a few more drinks then decided to check on Alan.

Knocking on his door he answered, "Yeah."

As I opened the door I said, "Hey partner, you ok?"

"Yeah, I just need to be alone for awhile."

"Ok. But if you need anything or just want to talk let me know."

"Yeah."

The next day the rest of our team arrived. We started a two day celebration of our reunion. We drank, snorted cocaine, and swapped war stories of what had happened over the last few months. Alan, however, spent most of the time in his room alone.

Over the next few months we all kept a low profile. The airways were filled with how the U.S. had sold arms to Iran and used the funds in a covert operation in Nicaragua. It also came out that the government was trading the arms sales to gain the release of political hostages. Soon Congress began holding hearings and calling in people that I thought would never surface, but they did. I wondered how much was known and how much would be released to the public. I also began to wonder if they knew the names of any of us peons and if they would try and call us.

I began to get a little edgy sitting around watching the hearings and getting wasted every day. I went to A.J. and said, "I need to get away for awhile."

"What you got in mind John?" He asked me.

"I thought I might take a week or so and go see my kids." I told him.

"I don't have a problem with that. Just be sure and keep me posted of how to reach you."

"Thanks A.J." I said.

Picking up the phone, I called the airlines and made reservations for the next morning. I then went to the bar and fixed two heavy, heavy scotches, went upstairs and knocked on Alan's door.

"Yeah."

"Hey it's me." I said struggling to open the door and handing him one of the drinks. "I brought you something."

"Thanks." He said in his depressed state as he accepted the drink.

"Hey, you ok man?" I asked.

"Yeah, sure." He answered.

"Listen, I'm leaving in the morning. I'm going to spend a week or so with my kids. You think you want to come along?"

"Nah."

"Hell, we could even go on up to Colorado and do some fishing." I prodded.

"Nah, uh uh."

"Aw come on, it'll be good for both of us."

"No! I said." He snapped back.

"Ok, ok. I'm just a little worried about you Alan."

"Don't be."

I left the next morning.

CHAPTER 53

I was enjoying the time away from Miami and even more enjoying my two sons. I watched them after school practice football and was in awe at how good they were and how big they were growing. After they finished their practice we did anything and everything they wanted.

Very early the morning of the fifth day, I was in my hotel room reading the local newspaper and drinking coffee when the phone rang. "Hello."

"John, this is A.J." Came the voice.

"Hey A.J. what's up?" I said.

"I need you back here ASAP." He said.

"ASAP? What the hells up, we got a big job or something?" I asked.

"You just need to get down here quick. Ok?"

"Alright." I shrugged. "I'll catch the first plane I can."

I called Linda and told here I wouldn't be able to pick the boys up because something had come up and I had to leave. I asked her to explain it to the boys and to promise them that it wouldn't be such a long period of time before I returned. Then I went to the airport and caught a flight to Miami.

When I arrived in Miami I quickly got a cab to the safe house. As I entered the house I was met by the whole team. Doug took my bag, Skip scurried off to fix me a drink and A.J. said "Come on in here John." As he followed Skip.

"What in the hell's going on here guys?" I asked with a half smile and following A.J. to the bar area.

A.J. took the glass of straight scotch from Skip and handed it to me, then said, "Here John, take a drink of this and sit down. I need to talk to you."

"Alright." I said as I took a pull from the glass then added, "Damn, this is strong, we run out of water?" As I set down I continued, "Come on now, what the hell's up? Am I in some kind of trouble or something?"

"No John." A.J. was struggling to talk. "John I wish I wasn't the one who had to tell you this, but," He took a pause pressing his lips tight together then, "Alan is dead."

My glass fell to the floor and time seemed to stop. "Bullshit. This isn't funny, don't joke like that." I yelled but really knowing it wasn't a joke.

Larry came over and put his hand on my shoulder and Skip began fixing me another drink as A.J. began, "It's no joke John, I wish it was. He shot himself last night."

Suddenly the words of the POW guard, during our escape, rang through my head, "They're all dead." Tears began to fill my eyes and my body started to tremble. I wanted to scream but my stomach was in my throat. The blood suddenly drained from my body and it felt like it was two hundred degrees in the room. Everything was hazy and confused like when I was first coming to after my crash when I was captured.

As A.J. was asking, "John, John you ok?" All I could do was look at him.

"Here buddy." Skip was saying, "Drink this," as he put the new glass of scotch in my hand.

"This can't be happening." I finally managed to mumble as I tried to slam down the scotch.

"He left this for you." A.J. was holding an envelope. "You feel like reading it now? Or you want it later?"

I grabbed the envelope and stared at it, afraid to open it. Maybe this was just a dream, I thought, but knew it wasn't.

I opened the envelope, took out the paper inside but tears made everything blurry. Wiping my eyes I began to read;

"John I know this is going to be hard on you, but I just can't take it any longer. Don't blame yourself for what I have done. I can't explain why I'm doing this other than it hurts to much to go on.

You always thought I was the strong one, but pal you were the strong one. I know it's a lot to put on you, but it's all up to you now and I know you can do it. You have to live for all eleven of us now.

John you were the closest thing in the world to me, closer than a brother could ever be. Remember me by the good times, not the misery.

Alan

P.S. Get out of the company."

I sat staring at the words wondering how I could go on now. Holding out my empty glass I said, "Please." Skip quickly took the glass to fix me another drink. Then I said, "I think I want to be alone now."

A.J. unsure of what my actions would be or what I may do said, "John we want to be with you. If you don't want to talk, that's alright, we'll just sit here."

"Here buddy." Skip said handing me a fresh drink. "John I just want to say, that," He started to choke up and everyone had tears in their eyes, "That we're all with you man. God I wish I knew what to say or do, but anything, anything."

"I guess I better make arrangements." I choked the words out cutting Skip off.

"Just relax." A.J. said. "Everything's being handled. The colonel's out right now, he'll take care of everything."

My legs were so rubbery during the funeral, I almost collapsed several times. A.J. and the others were always near me, holding me up and attempting to comfort me.

Once we returned to the safe house Doug fixed me a strong scotch and a line of cocaine. As I sat there I pulled out the letter, Alan had left, and once again tears filled my eyes. My emotions oscillated from sadness to anger, from love to hate, from pain to resentment.

210

"God damn it Alan, how could you do this to me?" So many thoughts and questions ran through my head. "Why do I have to be the one that has to carry on and live for all eleven of us?" "You promised me you wouldn't ever do this." "What the hell am I suppose to do now, you left me totally alone in the world?"

I sat there for the next day and a half drinking, snorting cocaine and thinking. I've never felt so lost and alone in all my life, including the time in the POW camp. Finally I asked A.J. for some extra cocaine, a lot extra. He looked at me a moment then nodded and rushed out of the room, returning with a large plastic bag, larger than a sandwich bag, and handed it to me, "What you going to do John?" I just shook my head.

I went upstairs to my room and put all my things in my bag. When I got to the bottom of the stairs A.J. stopped me, "John you're not going to do something stupid, are you?"

"I don't know. What's something stupid anyway?"

"Oh, John you know what I mean."

"A.J. if you mean, am I going to kill myself, no I guess not. I've got to live now for all eleven, I got to make the escape mean something." I said.

"You know that if there is anything you need or want, John we're, all of us, we're here for you. Where you going?" A.J. said.

"Right now I'm going to Colorado." I answered as A.J. squinted his eyes and looked inquisitively at me. "Good bye guys and thanks for everything." I finished as I walked out the door with my bag in hand and headed for a future of what I knew not. Right now however, I was going fishing.

Jerry Wood

ABOUT THE AUTHOR

Jerry Wood is a Vietnam veteran. He served in the United States Army from 1966 until 1975 as a helicopter pilot. While in the military he received numerous accommodations, awards and medals. Also while in the military he took correspondence courses and attended night school until he finally attained his BS degree.

Now living in South Florida, Jerry enjoys getting up early in the morning and writing while sitting by the ocean. He also enjoys sailing, scuba diving and golf.